Dan Mesa
Arizona Ranger

Dan Mesa Arizona Ranger

Dan Sears

iUniverse, Inc.
Bloomington

Dan Mesa Arizona Ranger

This is a work of fiction. All of the characters, names, incidents, organizations, and dialogue in this novel are either the products of the author's imagination or are used fictitiously.

iUniverse books may be ordered through booksellers or by contacting:

iUniverse
1663 Liberty Drive
Bloomington, IN 47403
www.iuniverse.com
1-800-Authors (1-800-288-4677)

ISBN: 978-1-4620-3285-3 (sc)
ISBN: 978-1-4620-3287-7 (hc)
ISBN: 978-1-4620-3286-0 (ebk)

Printed in the United States of America

iUniverse rev. date: 08/03/2011

ACKNOWLEDGMENTS

This book is a work of fiction. What is written is from the imagination of the writer. If any event in this book is similar to an actual incident, then it is purely coincidental. The Arizona Rangers still exist, but in reality they are not a law enforcement agency. They are men and women who are willing and able to respond when called upon by local law enforcement agencies. Chapter 40, Article 41 of Legislative Act 41, signed into law April 30, 2003, specifically explains the role of the Arizona Rangers. The act is mentioned in this story because of those who will question the Rangers' law enforcement capabilities.

This book is dedicated to the original "Twenty-Six Men" who were the original Arizona Rangers, the present-day Arizona Rangers, and the men and women wearing the badge and enforcing the law. Also, if by chance I accidentally used someone's material and did not acknowledge that person, I most humbly apologize for my oversight.

To my friend Sam Jones

INTRODUCTION

If you are reading this book, it has been published. I want to tell you about the main character in this book, whose name is Daniel Mesa, better known as Dan Mesa. I'm Captain Sam Johnson of the Arizona Rangers stationed at Nogales, Arizona. Sergeant Dan Mesa is assigned to the Santa Cruz Detachment in Nogales. I have known Dan since 1994, when he retired from the air force and was teaching at Nogales High School. There was an attempted robbery of one of our local banks, and one of the Rangers was shot. Mesa just happened to be passing by and saw the Ranger as he was shot. Mesa, being who he is, went to assist the Ranger. The Ranger deputized Mesa and told him to stop the bank robber.

Now the story is taken over by Anna Herrera, who said, "I was in the bank with the robber when this fellow walked in with a badge on his chest. He just looked at the robber and said, 'Fella, you've got two choices: drop that gun or die where you stand. Which will it be?'

"The robber spun around and fired at the man with the badge, but he was already moving, and firing his weapon as he moved. He hit the robber once in the shoulder, making him drop the gun. The robber grabbed for me, but the fella with the gun shot him twice (one bullet caught him in the chest and the other in the head), and he was dead. I later learned that the man with the gun was the Air Force ROTC teacher at our high school. I'm glad he was there."

When we arrived on the scene, I saw a small man tending to our Ranger, who had been shot. The fellow in question looked at me and said, "You look as if you are the one in charge, so I guess I'd better tell you what happened."

He told me of his involvement in the shooting and never left out a word. When he finished, he asked if there was anything he could do for the Ranger and I said "No, but thanks for everything." He turned to leave and I thought to myself, "This fella would make an excellent Ranger."

"Excuse me, sir, but have you ever thought about becoming a Ranger? The pay is good and the benefits are good. It is dangerous, as you can see, but it is fun."

He looked at me with a bit of a twinkle in his eye and said, "What do I have to do?"

"Well, you will have to attend the police academy, graduate, and then you will be assigned to me. Do you think you'd like a try at it?"

"Yes, sir, I'd like nothing better. When and where do I report?"

"The next class will start in two months; can you be ready to start by then?"

"The only thing I have to do is resign from my job at the high school. Captain, thanks for the opportunity, and I promise I won't let you down."

Dan Mesa graduated at the top of his class in 1995, went to work for the Rangers, and has made the Rangers very proud of him. `

DAN MESA ARIZONA RANGER

Sometimes I wonder how my life would have turned out if I had chosen a different path. If I had not joined the air force and remained a teacher, would it have turned out differently, or was this my destiny all along? Having this pain inside and lying here in the hospital room gives me time to think on how I got to this point. It all began about a month ago.

Captain Johnson sends for me and says, "Dan, I want you to arrest one José Gutierrez-Jackson. He robbed a Wells Fargo Truck in El Paso last week and escaped with five hundred thousand dollars and killed two of the guards.
He is also wanted by the state of Texas for armed robbery and murder. Bring him in dead or alive but preferably alive."

"Sir, as you are aware, I know José quite well, and we were friends at one time. Are you sure you want me to go after him?"

"Dan, there are a lot of things said about you, some complimentary and some not so complimentary, but no one has ever said you were dishonest or lacking in integrity. I know that you will do the right thing so I'm not worried.}
"

"Okay, sir, I will get started. Do you have the warrant and necessary papers for me to arrest him?"

The captain gives me the warrant and other papers. "Sergeant, don't take any chances with José. He is not the same man he was when you were friends. He's changed, and he'll kill you just like he would any other person. He has gone bad."

The captain is right. I have followed Jackson since we did our thing down on the border. Something made him change and turn bad, and he has gone bad all the way. He is a tough customer and will not be taken easily. Killing those two guards wasn't necessary. That was just pure meanness. It is right that I am the one to go after him. The question is, can I kill a man who was once my friend? Yes, if necessary!

I have a feeling this is going to be a long and dangerous endeavor. Being prepared and ready is paramount. I need my sleeping bag and camping equipment, along with MREs—meals ready to eat. I'll need my .357 Magnum, hunting rifle, one hundred rounds of ammo for each one, my derringer, and my hunting knife. Oh yes, my first aid and survival kit. I'll need my oilcloth coat and liner just in case the weather changes. I will carry my bulletproof vest also, and water and coffee and some cigars. I'll also need matches. I'll use the Toyota for this trip; it is four-wheel drive and will go just about anyplace. I've had it for ten years and took it overseas to the Persian Gulf. It is a solid old truck, and I will probably keep it a bit longer, although that four-cylinder engine lacks power. I guess I have everything I will need.

"Captain, I'm ready to depart. Where do you want me to start looking for José?"

"You should probably start here in Nogales," he says.

"Sir, I believe he has a lady friend working at the Cow Palace in Amado, and I'd like to start there."

I have always liked Amado; it reminds me of days gone by. It was the favorite watering hole of many actors and actresses who frequented the area. The actor Stewart Granger once owned a ranch in the area of Nogales, near the golf course. John Wayne hung around the area making movies in the fifties and sixties. Even Clint Eastwood and Whoopie Goldberg visited the area. Amado has an interesting history. Amado and Nogales are neighboring towns with interesting histories. I also enjoy the drive. We are here.

I should probably ask if Sylvia is working.   "Excuse me, ma'am; I'm Sergeant Dan Mesa of the Arizona Rangers. Can you tell me if Sylvia Animas is working this evening?"

"Ranger, I am Maria and you need to talk with Sonia,. She can tell you what you want to know. I will get her."

"Sonia, there is a Ranger out there in the bar looking for Sylvia." Sonia looks at Maria with surprise and says; "OK you stay here in the dining room and I'll talk with the Ranger."

"Martha, be serious. There aren't any Rangers left in Arizona. They only exist in Texas."

"Sonia, I don't know about Texas, but there is a real-life, honest-to-goodness Ranger standing in the bar and asking questions. See for yourself."

"Sir, may I help you? I am Sonia Perdenales, and I own the bar. I understand you are looking for Sylvia Animas. May I ask why?"

"Yes, ma'am. I'm Ranger Dan Mesa from the Santa Cruz Company in Nogales. I'm looking for José Gutierrez-Jackson, an acquaintance of Miss Animas. José is wanted for armed robbery of a Wells Fargo armored truck and for killing two guards. He may decide to head this way."

"Okay, Ranger, I will get her for you she is on break. I know José, and he can be a dangerous person, so you should be careful also." She returns with Sylvia.

"Ranger, I understand you want to talk to me about José. I haven't seen him in over two months. José knows not to come around when he's in trouble with the law."

"Ma'am, if he does come to see you, tell him I was here asking about him, and he knows I am looking for him. If you tell him what I have said that will prevent you from having any trouble with him. I thank you for talking with me. Is it possible to get a table? I'd like to eat dinner since I am here."

Miss Perdenales returns and asks, "Ranger, would you like a drink? It's on the house."
"No, ma'am. I'm still on duty, but I would like to have dinner."

She seats me in the restaurant and a waiter comes by. I order a steak with rice, green beans, tomatoes, and iced tea. I notice an older gentleman watching very closely, and finally he speaks.

He says, "Excuse me, sir, but exactly what branch of law enforcement are you?"

"Sir, I am with the Arizona Rangers, Santa Cruz Company of Nogales."

"I didn't know you guys still existed! No one ever hears anything about you."

"Well, sir, we are still in existence and we still enforce the law. We primarily work from the governor's office on capital crimes. When you see us, someone has violated a federal or state law."

Then a lady says, "Sergeant, you are about the best-looking thing I have seen in pants in a very long time." Now, what do you say to a

4

comment like that?. Miss Perdenales who witnessed this exchange is standing there and smiling at me. Suddenly it has gotten very warm in here.

The waiter returns and I order coffee. I really like this place. It reminds me of some other places I have been in over the years. He brings the bill, and I leave a tip and prepare to leave.As I depart, Miss Perdenales says, "Ranger, come back for a visit when you are not on duty, and have a drink. It'll still be on the house."

"Thank you, ma'am. I will do that. I like the atmosphere and the people here."

She shakes my hand, deposits a piece of paper in it, and smiles. I must admit that her smile makes me want to smile. It has been said that I don't smile enough and am unfriendly. I don't necessarily agree with that opinion of me. It is also said that I resemble George Jefferson, and I don't agree with that either.

Now, back to Nogales and to get ready for tomorrow. I have a feeling it is going to be an interesting day. I have gone over everything in my mind to make sure I am ready to challenge Jackson. One or both of us will be hurt before this is over. Jackson is a crack shot, and so am I. I hope it doesn't come down to him or me. I had to take a life before, and it did not sit well with me. Killing is easy, but living with what you have done is a different story. I hate the thought of killing José, but I will do it if it is necessary.

It is time for bed and a good night's sleep. Oh yes, what was that paper that Miss Perdenales gave me? Let's see—it's her phone number and address. I was half hoping that was what she gave me. She is a beautiful woman, but it has been a long time since I have been interested in anyone. After my wife left me, I gave up on love and everything related to it and just concentrated on work. I have missed out on a lot over the last two years. I miss my son; he is my life these days. When my wife left, it just tore me apart for a while. I never understood what tore us apart. That is something for another day. Today is Wednesday or Wednesday night. I wonder how long this will take.

I awaken from a dream. The bad dreams are back. I haven't had them for a while. I guess it is because of the stress I place on myself. Breakfast, and then it's time to hit the road.

"Captain, I visited Amado and talked with an old girlfriend of Jackson, but she hasn't seen him. He does have friends in Sierra Vista. I believe it would be a good idea to go to Sierra Vista and nose around a bit."

"Sergeant, you be careful. José is not the same person he was fifteen years ago. He has changed—and not for the better. He will kill you if he has to. I don't want to go to a funeral anytime soon."

"I agree with you, sir, and I will be careful. There is too much I haven't done or seen yet, and I want to see my son again. I will talk with you soon."

A quick check to see if I have all the equipment I need: my guns, ammo, knife, food, first aid kit, and the warrant. Highway 87 to Patagonia. Oh yes, I forgot, Jackson has friends in Patagonia. I had best notify Marshal Huitt to be on the lookout for Jackson. "Sergeant Mesa to headquarters."

"Go ahead, Sergeant. This is headquarters."

"Yes, the suspect Jackson has friends in Patagonia. Please notify Marshal Huitt and have him be on the lookout for Jackson. Please let him know that Jackson is armed and extremely dangerous. Mesa out."

Patagonia is an interesting town. I like the sidewalks and buildings; they remind me of a different time period. There is a hotel there that serves a really good breakfast, and the scenery isn't bad either. We have Ranger Day celebrations in Patagonia sometimes. It is a quaint little town and a good place to live. The drive between Nogales and Patagonia can be deceptive it is longer than it appears to be due to the scenery. Holy Hanna, there goes Jackson! He is headed into Washington Camp which is an old abandon silver mine. Once he's in that area, we'll never get him out. That place is a series of hiding places and a straight route to the border. There are places along the border where there aren't any patrols or sensors and crossing the border is not a problem. If Jackson gets into Mexico, we will never see him again. The idea is to prevent his escape.

There, I see his truck. I know José, and there is a good chance he has a surprise for me somewhere out here. It looks as if Jackson is headed toward the old mine. There are many different areas to hide or ambush a person from out here. I am going to stop here and track for a while. I have that old feeling again—the one that tells me I am being watched. It is amazing how you revert to being like an animal in the wild when the challenge is put before you. Jackson is close by, and I can feel his eyes watching me. I had better grab my rifle. I have a feeling I will need it. I'd better find some cover, because standing here exposed is not a good idea.

He could be behind any rock or tree. There are many places to hide. What was that? I do believe someone is shooting at me! "José, this is Dan Mesa of the Arizona Rangers. I am here to arrest you for armed robbery and murder."

"Dan, ain't this a *bitch*. You sent to arrest me? Couldn't they have sent someone else? Amigo, things are not what they used to be. Times have changed."

"José, they sent me because we were friends at one time, and they figured that if anyone could get you to surrender without a shootout, it would be me. So, amigo, what's it going to be?"

7

"Dan, I can't surrender, and I am not going back to jail. I robbed Wells Fargo and I killed two guards, so the death penalty is staring me in the face."

"José, you could be right, but that is not my department. I want to take you in before others get hurt or killed. José, José, are you there?" That fellow can be somewhat abrupt. When he stops talking, he starts shooting. There it is.

That rifle has a wicked bite to it. This is starting to make me very angry. It is time to return fire, but what do I shoot at? This is not acceptable. José had better make sure he doesn't hit my truck. I guess he has escaped. Time to move. I am fair at tracking, so let's see where he has gone. Those tracks are of a man in sneakers with worn soles. He is headed toward Sierra Vista using these back roads. As I recall, there are several trails that lead into Mexico, and they are not guarded either. If Jackson gets into Mexico, we will never get him back, so I must attempt to prevent him from crossing over. Time to scat. That old Ram Charger is a heck of a vehicle and will go anyplace, but so will mine. He has twice the horsepower, though, and that makes a difference. Now what?

This isn't good. It looks like he has set a trap for me. An abandoned vehicle with the engine running and the doors open. "Warning: Approach with Caution." Common sense says circle around, try to get a feel for what is going on, and use caution. I have great common sense, and I don't like this one bit. "Jackson, this isn't going to work. You're only making it harder for yourself." Now, where did that guy go? He is a very dangerous person, especially when he is cornered. José, you are starting to make me very angry, and that's not good. Where the hell are you?

I've been in this position before in Vietnam in 1975. I didn't like it then and I don't like it now. This puts one in a death-wish position. If I try to get closer, I will have to expose myself to his fire. Now what do I do? Common sense says to be extremely careful and cautious. My best bet is to return to my truck and block the road with it. Now, to ease myself back to my truck. Oops, there he goes in that bloody Ram Charger. I had better hurry and follow him. I'd say that given the direction he is heading, he is either crossing over into Mexico or heading for Sierra Vista. There are several back trails you can follow into Mexico without having to cross over at the official border crossings. If he gets into Mexico, we will never catch him. Now, how do I stop him from crossing the border? I'll have to try to shoot his tires out, which is a dangerous proposition from my standpoint. I'll try to get in front of him and force him to turn around. This old truck sometimes surprises me. I actually am able to get in front of that Ram Charger and force him to turn. YES! Now, to chase him to Sierra Vista. I had better give Marshal Huitt a call.

"Marshal Huitt, this is Ranger Mesa from Santa Cruz Company and I am in hot pursuit of one José Gutierrez-Jackson, wanted for armed robbery and murder. He is headed in your direction. I'll be there in about fifteen minutes. Please have your deputies be on the watch for him. He's driving a Dodge Ram Charger, black in color with the slogan Born to Be Bad written on it. Please approach with caution. He is very dangerous."

I am in Patagonia and knowing Jose as I do, he will probably stop off here just to throw me off his trail. Now to find the marshal. I see him. "Marshal Huitt, have you seen or heard anything from Jackson yet?" He answers no but believes he may have seen José's truck, although he's not sure. There goes Jackson now!

"Dan, I am going to try to force him to surrender. This is my town, and I don't want a shootout in my streets."

"Marshal, Jackson is dangerous. Don't take any chances with him. He will kill you." Darn, no one wants to listen. He is going to get himself killed or get hurt very badly. "Marshal Huitt, duck!" Oh, no! Jackson just shot Huitt and now all manners of Hade are going to break loose.

"Captain Johnson, Mesa here. Jackson shot Marshal Huitt, and he isn't expected to live. I returned fire but only managed to shoot his boot heel off."

"Sergeant Mesa, I want Jackson stopped and I don't care how you do it! He has killed two and possibly three people. This is getting out of hand. If you can't do the job, I will get someone else to do it. Do you understand me?"

"Sir, I will do my best. If Marshal Huitt had listened to me, he wouldn't have been shot. He wanted to arrest Jackson himself, and that was a mistake. Jackson will not be arrested peacefully, and it will take someone like me to arrest him. He knows I can and will shoot to kill."

"Sergeant, I suggest you get started!"

Jackson will move on to Sierra Vista, and I will try to take him there. "Mesa to headquarters."

"Headquarters, go ahead."

"Notify Sierra Vista police to be on the lookout for Jackson. He has friends there, and I'm positive he'll show up there. Mesa out."

Jackson will probably visit the Cordon Bleu to see a favorite friend of his. The Cordon Bleu is a nice motel, but it is more than a motel. It is a man's place. It is a brothel. The lady who runs the place is a "The lady who runs the place is a real lady." I have known her for a few years, and she is okay in my book. There are probably those who would point fingers, but not me. She helped me make it through the nights after my wife left with my son. I owe her a debt I can never repay. She saved my life. However, that is another story. Sierra Vista is the location of Fort Huachuca, a historic army fort, and the original home of the Buffalo Soldiers. It holds meaning for me because of a distant cousin who served in the unit during the

Indian Wars and also during World War I. Sierra Vista is not very large. As a matter of fact it is a quaint little town that is just the right place to live in peace. Ah . . . the Cordon Bleu.

"Good evening, ladies. I am looking for Ms. Olivetti. Please tell her Dan Mesa of the Arizona Rangers would like to speak to her." I can hear them in the back. Someone is saying, "Janie, there's a guy with a badge who says he's an Arizona Ranger."

Another voice says, "What is his name and what does he look like?"

"Janie, he is colored and handsome, with a sad face. He says he's Dan Mesa. The name *Mesa* is Hispanic, isn't it?"

"Yes, it is, and Dan is one person in a million. I wouldn't let him hear you call him colored. He has a dislike for that word and the *N* word."

She enters, and my goodness, she hasn't changed at all during these past few years. "Hello, Daniel," she says.

"Hello, Janie. It's been a few years, but you look the same—only more beautiful." "Dan, you've changed some. Your face is sadder, but darn, you are handsome. What have you been doing with yourself since I saw you last?"

It's hard to answer her question. "I've adjusted to my place in the scheme of things and am trying to get on with my life. I owe you a debt I'll never be able to repay. You saved my life, and I'll never forget it."

"Thanks, but you didn't come here for that," she says. "I can tell by the way you look. What is it?"

11

"Janie, it's José. He robbed a Wells Fargo truck and killed two guards. Then he shot Marshal Huitt over in Patagonia, and he's dead, too. José has turned bad, and he's armed and dangerous. Have any of the ladies seen him today?" She explains to me that one of the ladies had a relationship with Jackson until he became abusive.

Jackson is changing. I remember a time when he would never have abused a lady and would have killed anyone who did. He is changing, and he needs to be stopped. "Janie, I am going to try to stop José before some other person is shot. I better head over to the police station. I'll be back soon, unless all hell breaks loose.OK. I believe I'll call the police instead.

"Captain Heath, this is Sergeant Mesa of the Arizona Rangers, Santa Cruz Company. I'm searching for one José Gutierrez-Jackson, who is wanted for robbery of a Wells Fargo truck and the murder of two guards, and the murder of Marshal Huitt in Patagonia. He is en route to Sierra Vista and may be here as we speak. Please advise your patrols to be on the watch for Jackson.

"He's armed and extremely dangerous. Please advise your patrols not to attempt to apprehend him alone. I believe I can talk him into giving up or at least prevent anyone from getting shot or killed."

"Sergeant, no son of a bitch is going to come into my city and take over as long as I am police chief. Now, as for you Rangers, you are just a bunch of out-of-date dinosaurs. I thank you, but we can do our own arresting."

"Captain, you and your people may be good, but I tell you, Jackson is better. But have it your own way. Before this day is over, at least one or two of your men will be dead or seriously injured."

I know it is time to hang up before I say more than is needed. Jackson is here. I feel his presence, and I know he is here. I'd better walk around town and stay close by the Cordon Bleu. He may attempt to contact one of the girls. There was a time when I would have taken offense at the captain's remarks about the Rangers, but I am older now, and words don't hurt that much anymore. It's almost 6:00 p.m., and I haven't eaten since breakfast. I should probably eat while I can. I saw a cozy little restaurant around the corner. I hope they have fish. I have a craving for trout or salmon. I wish I enjoyed cooking as some do, but for me it is a serious chore. I remember the food from Turkey and how simple it was for them to prepare a meal. We in the West make it so difficult. I am here, and it appears to be clean and the smell is appealing. "Yes, may I have the baked trout with green beans, sweet potatoes, and rice? Also, may I have both lemonade and coffee to drink?"

Now I must find Jackson. I still feel his presence and I know he is here. I'll check back at the Cordon Bleu. There he goes! "Ranger Mesa to police headquarters. Jackson is headed down First Street driving a black Ram Charger four-by-four. Remember, he is dangerous. Use all cover and concealment." Someone is going to die tonight. Well, all hell is breaking loose. The police are attempting to block him in. "Captain, your people are going to get someone killed. You can't stop him using those tactics! He is going to start shooting and someone is going to be hurt."

"Ranger, I told you we can handle our own problems, so butt out and we will take care of Jackson."

That patrolman is trying to force him into a trap. That is not the way to handle this situation. Oh, my goodness, Jackson just shot that patrolman. "Captain Heath, you have just lost a patrolman. Now will you please listen to me? Let him go for now, because if you don't, there will be more dead people than you can bury. Take care of that patrolman. He is more important than fifty Jacksons. Call your men off and notify the state police." I am going after Jackson. He has to be stopped one way or another. At this point I believe the only way to stop him is to kill him. "Sergeant Mesa to headquarters, over."

"Go ahead, Sergeant, this is Ranger Malloy."

"Malloy, tell the captain that Jackson has killed a policeman in Sierra Vista. This time he committed murder and there were several witnesses.""Dan, this is Captain Johnson, what happened, over?"

"Sir, all hell has broken loose here. Captain Heath refused to let me help and approached the situation in the wrong way, and he caused the death of one of his policemen. Captain, I need to report in and bring you up to date before this gets blown out of proportion. Someone is going to be in trouble because of this, and I don't want it to be us."

"Dan, tie up all loose ends there and report in sometime tomorrow. Your report has to be detailed, leaving out nothing, do you understand?"

"Yes, sir, I do. I'll see you tomorrow."I need to try and set things straight with Captain Heath. "Sir, I have been ordered back to Nogales. But before I go, is there anything I can do for you?"

"Yes, Ranger kill that animal before he kills anyone else. Send him straight to hell for me! I have to tell that patrolman's wife who is my sister, that her husband and the father of their three kids will not be coming home ever again. His name was Franco Alvarez, and he was a nice guy who should not be dead. What do I say to my sister and the kids?"

"You can tell her that Ranger Dan Mesa said Jackson will pay for his sins, I promise you that. Captain, take care of your people. We will be in touch."

It is always the same when a cop is killed. We all want revenge, but you can't become the judge, jury, and executioner. Our job is to serve and protect, and when the law goes bad, everyone loses. It is sad any day when a policeman is killed, but it's doubly sad in this case because he leaves children behind who need their father. I feel a tinge of guilt because I am alive and he isn't. How can this be? This whole thing needs to end. Today is Thursdaythe second day since I started tracking Jackson. Jackson has killed two people in two days and four since this thing s began last week. I've got to get him out in the open. Time to head back to Nogales and report in.

"Captain, I'm back and I've completed my report. It's on this disk. I've included everything I can think of that is relative to the case. Sir, if I may say so, this last shooting could have been prevented if Captain Heath had listened to me. He was obstinate and refused help, and he paid a heavy price for it. The patrolman who was shot was his brother-in-law. I do not envy him in what he has to do. That policeman should still be alive. Sir, I made a promise to his family, and I plan to keep that promise. I promised them I would bring Jackson in dead or alive. Either way, he will pay for his sins. I have got to stop him. A person can't do what he has done and get away with it. He shot Marshal Huitt in Patagonia, and less than twelve hours later he killed a policeman in a town less than a hundred miles away. He isn't rational anymore. He told me when I cornered him in Washington Camp that he wasn't going back to jail and knew he was headed toward death row. He plans to go out in a hail of bullets, and he plans to take a few of us along with him."

"Sergeant, Jackson will be taken out one way or another, but I don't want you to get yourself killed tackling him. What do you think his next move will be?"

"Sir, I believe he will stop off here and then head toward Yuma. He has a host of relatives and friends there, and they will attempt to protect him. As I recall he has three brothers and a sister in Yuma plus at least fifteen cousins. They are tough and meaner than a scalded snake. Captain, it would be to our advantage to notify the police in Yuma and the Ranger Company there. I am going to eventually need their help."

"There is a bar right here in Nogales called Los Negritos where he used to hang out. I'll check in there. I'll need backup, because even though they know me, they also know I'm after Jackson, and they won't help me at all. In English, the name of the bar means 'the black people.' Jackson does have African-American blood. His grandfather was black—thus the name Jackson. I need two people, but send only people who know how to fight dirty. I'm going to get some sleep and will be in around six o'clock tomorrow morning to finish up some of the paperwork from that drug case last week."

"Okay, Dan, but get some sleep. You look as if you need it. And don't come in at six—I'll see you around eight. That is an order, okay?"

"Understood, sir."

Well, home again, such as it is. One of these days I am going to finish that barn. I should put in a concrete flow with a sewage drain. But there is something about having a dirt floor in a barn and the smell of it all. I guess I just like horses. I like them even better than I like most people.

I should call Sonia. I am really afraid of being turned down—although she did give me her number, so I assume she wants to be called. Here goes. The phone is ringing.

"Hello, ma'am, this is Ranger Mesa. We met at the Cow Palace a couple of days ago"

"Yes, Ranger, I remember you. I'd begun to think I was never going to hear from you. But I'm so happy that you decided to call. How have you been, and why did it take so long for you to call?"

"I must apologize for not calling sooner, but the case I am working on has taken a serious turn for the worse. After leaving you that evening I followed Jackson to Patagonia, where he shot and killed the marshal, and from there to Sierra Vista, where he killed a policeman. Now I believe he is here in Nogales."

"Dan—may I call you Dan?"

"Yes, ma'am, that is what most people call me. However, my name is Daniel. I'm French Creole on my father's side."

"Daniel, I'm glad you called. I know what I did seemed very forward, but sometimes when you see something you like, you have to go after it—or in this case, go after him, meaning you. I like you, and I have from the first moment I saw you. My husband was killed in the line of duty. He was a policeman in a small town in Colorado, and while answering an alarm, he was shot and killed. It happened five years ago, and it has taken that much time to get over it. I guess I have a soft spot for cops."

"Ma'am, I mean, Sonia, if you have some free time tomorrow, how about having breakfast with me?"

"Dan, I'd rather have dinner with you tomorrow night if you are free. I'd like to spend a few hours getting to know you, that is, if it's possible to get to know you. I believe you have a lot of things filed away in your psyche that aren't ready to be talked about, but that is something for another day." I can sense that she is smiling by the sound of her voice.

I like this lady!

"Yes, I'd like to have dinner with you. I'll make sure I'm free tomorrow night. Well, I'll call you later tomorrow. Good night."

Now to get a shower and some sleep. I hope for an uninterrupted sleep without nightmares.

Today is Friday and these reports have to be finished before noon. There is a bar right here in Nogales called Los Negritos where Jose hung out.

"Captain, I think we should roust Los Negritos around two o'clock this afternoon in our search for Jackson. I think we should take John Swank, Mike Savalas, and Bonefacio Hernandez. Also, we should require everyone to put on his or her vest and be prepared for whatever happens. This isn't going to be a cake walk."

This place looks dangerous even from the outside. A lot of blood has flowed on the floor, and a lot of lives have been influenced by what has happened here. It should be closed down, but it is one of those historical places. It was built in the 1800s and has an interesting history. It has been said that the Tenth Calvary spent time drinking and carousing here.

"Ladies and gentlemen, this is a raid, so everyone put your hands on the bar and don't move. Please, don't do anything to get yourself killed. I am Sergeant Mesa of the Rangers, and we are looking for José Gutierrez-Jackson. I know you know him, so let's get to issues. If you see him, tell him Dan Mesa of the Rangers is looking for him."

As I turn to leave a customer says, "Señor, why you hassling us poor peons? We work hard all day, drink a little beer in the evenings, and party, man. So why you hassling us? We don't break any laws and we don't want anything from you guys."

"Sir, I don't want anything from you, either," I say. "I just want Jackson. He is wanted for four murders: two in Texas and two here in Arizona, all policemen. Now, if you help us, we'll help you by leaving and not bothering you. So, what will it be?"

"I am Pepe and I don't like you Rangers, so it's going to be me kicking your butt out of here. What do you say to that?"

"I hoped we could do this without a fight, but have it your way."

I hate to fight, but believe me, I know how to fight and I do fight dirty. That fellow over there has a broken nose and possibly two shattered ribs. The black gentleman has a busted lip and a few other bruises. It appears John and Bonefacio have their hands full. "Fella, you are about to get yourself killed unless you drop that knife. I won't tell you a second time."

This fella must be crazy; he's coming after me with that bloody knife. I'd better act quickly before he kills me. I've always been fast, but killing still comes hard for me. I've had to kill before, but I honestly hate hurting anyone. If he had listened, he'd still be alive.

"Okay, this fight is over, so settle down. Now, would you like to tell us where Jackson is or should we come back every day until we drive your customers away and drive you out of business? What will it be?"

"Ranger, you made your point. José was here and left just before you arrived. You didn't see him because he changed vehicles. He's driving a Dodge Durango four-by-four. It's red with an eagle painted on the rear. Now how about it? Let us get back to partying."

"Okay, we're out of here. Next time make it easier on yourself and cooperate with the police."

As I enter the Captain's office he says in a loud voice, "Sergeant Mesa! What in the good blue blazes happened at that bar?
Has the whole flaming world gone nuts? All I want to do is apprehend José Gutierrez-Jackson and get him off the streets. At least you didn't kill anyone. You only wounded him. What happened?"

"Sir, I did have to shoot and I did kill a fellow, but it was in the line of duty. Captain Johnson, we went in as nice as you please, but one loudmouth decided he didn't like Rangers and wanted to kick our butts, and that wasn't an option. I don't like getting my butt kicked by anyone, so I took the lead and kicked his first. None of us were injured, and at this point that is what I am most concerned about. We've lost too many cops in these last few days. Captain, I know this case is an accident looking for a place to happen, but we are just being stopped at every turn. We'll get our chance soon. I feel it in my bones. Jackson will slip up, and I will be there. He has changed vehicles and is driving a red Dodge Durango with an eagle painted on the rear. I think we should send out an all-points bulletin with Jackson's description and a description of his vehicle. Also, ask the governor to offer a reward of, say, five thousand dollars for any information leading to his capture. We will get some action then. Four cases of murder make him a very dangerous fellow."

"Dan, you have a point. This will keep the governor's office off our back and give Senator Ibarra something to do besides kick us around. Do you know that that man and his family still hold the Rangers responsible for his great-uncle's death in 1904? That was ninety-six years ago, and he still holds a grudge. I still get angry over that. All right, I'll contact the colonel and ask for the reward. Dan, you did a good job overall. Now, a lady named Sonia Perdenales called and wanted to talk to you. She sounds very nice. Her name was mentioned in one of your reports. Anyway, she seemed to have a very high opinion of you. Sergeant, it is time for you bounce back from your marriage problems and find a life again. I know I'm overstepping my authority, but this is just an opinion from a friend. Ask that lady out on a date and enjoy life again. I still see that torn side of you. You are the best Ranger I ever worked with, but you need a social life also." I could tell he was smiling as he said that. "Now go and have some fun."

"Thank you, sir."

"Colonel Grant, Captain Johnson from Santa Cruz Company. I'm calling about the José Gutierrez-Jackson situation."

"Hello, Sam, it's good to hear from you. I've read all of your reports on Jackson. I think it is time to play hardball. I have been given the authority to offer a reward of ten thousand dollars for any information leading to his capture. What do you think?"

"I think that's great. As a matter of fact I was calling to ask you to do just that. Thanks, sir."

"Sam, Dan Mesa is a hell of a Ranger. Please him tell I said so. He makes me wish I were still in the field. He has good instinct and he knows just how far to go and how much force to use. I know he has a temper and I also know about his personal problems. How is he handling it?"

"Colonel, he recovered from the drinking a year or so ago and works harder than ever. The breakup took a toll on him and he compensates by working too hard. I just gave him an order to go out and have some fun. I think there may be a lady coming into his life. I met his wife once. Garnett is a nice lady but a little too headstrong. She hates the West and the job he has. So she moved back east and took the boy, and that was too much for him to take. He has been through two wars and carries the scars from both, but even that didn't throw him like she did. It's an odd situation."

"Okay, Sam, you have my support. Keep me informed and capture that son of a bitch!"

"Thanks, sir, I will."

Dan Mesa, what have you gotten yourself into? What does that lady want with a broken-down old Ranger like you? Sometimes I still feel Garnett and Devlin's presence. It has been three years, three months, and ten days since she left. The captain is right. I need to get a life.

"Sonia, Dan Mesa here. I'm calling to find out if you're still free for dinner tonight."

"Hello, Ranger, it's good to hear your voice again. It's all over the news about the raid you carried out in Nogales at Los Negritos. I am so happy you weren't injured. Yes, I'm still available, and dinner and dancing will be great. I haven't danced since Charlie's death."

"Great! I'll pick you up around 7 p.m."I have messages, one from my brother David, one from Mom, and one from Devlin. I hope all is well there. What the hell was that? Someone just shot through my window! This is ridiculous! It reminds me of the Gulf War."Ranger headquarters, Ranger Mendosa speaking."

"Mendosa, Sergeant Mesa here. Someone just shot into my house. Please send out an investigative team and the police. Also, notify Captain Johnson. They also shot one of my horses. Whoever did this will pay a healthy price for their actions."

"Dan, tell me what happened."

"Sir, I do believe someone was trying to take me out. I must be getting too close, or someone who was at that bar is seeking revenge. They shot one of my horses also, and that does make me angry. That horse has been my friend for ten years. I think they were trying to scare me off, but I just don't frighten very easily, and someone is going to pay dearly for this."

Captain Johnson and the police have arrived and are checking the place over, looking for evidence. The crime scene guys are very thorough.

"Dan, do you have any idea who did this?"

"Sir, I believe it was José trying to scare me off. He has failed, but I won't fail. He will pay for killing my horse.""Dan, don't do anything rash, okay? Now, go on and take that nice young lady to dinner. We'll finish up here. Make sure you're armed, and don't get careless."

Sonia lives in a nice area. I've been here before. I don't particularly like mobile homes, but one does what one can.

"Hello, Dan. It is good to see you again. I wasn't quite sure what to wear, so I chose this pants suit. It's not too dressy but not too casual either. What do you think?"

"Ma'am, I think you are beautiful and the outfit only enhances your overall self. I do believe you'd look great in whatever you wore. I really like your perfume. It has a nice aroma but it's not too heavy."

"Okay, Dan, I've embarrassed you enough. I just wanted to see if you could express your feelings, and you pass with flying colors." She smiles. "Now, where are we going? If you don't mind, I'd like to go to a nice place where there is dining and dancing. I know of a place in Tucson that isn't very expensive."

"Well, I made reservations at Clancy's, which is a very nice place with dining and dancing. But I can cancel if you'd like."

"No, Dan, that's the place I was thinking of. I just didn't think it was a place you'd be familiar with—and I don't mean that in a mean way."

"Sonia, I used to go there when I was stationed here back in the eighties. I like the place, and they usually have a band playing big band music and western music. Are you ready to go?"

"You know something? I have been worried about tonight, because I wasn't sure you'd like me. I thought I was too much of a country girl, and some guys like all that fluff and glitz."

"Sonia, you look absolutely beautiful, and I am the one who was frightened about going out with you. But I think we can both relax and enjoy the evening. I'm a good dancer when it involves slow dancing and country dancing. I promise I won't step on your feet," I add, smiling.I really enjoy the drive between Nogales and Tucson. There is so much of this country I enjoy. It reminds me of Turkey. I was stationed there during and after the Gulf War. It has cactus and desert and lots of open space like we have here in Arizona. I really love the Southwest and never want to leave. Arizona is one of the few places where I feel as though I belong. People here have accepted me as I am for the most part. I love the people and the food, and the ladies are most beautiful.

"Dan, I get the feeling that took courageyou to verbalize. On behalf of the people of Arizona, I thank you, sir."My son asked why I didn't live with him and his mom. He said, 'Daddy, why do you live so far away? Don't you like Mommy and me?' I didn't know how to answer him. I just said, 'Son, you mean more to me than anything, and I love your mom dearly, but I am not so sure she feels the same."

"Since that conversation, I've thought about moving east, but what will I do there? I don't fit into that environment. I like being a Ranger and everything that goes with it. It is dangerous, the job I do, but I find a lot of contentment and a sense of accomplishment in it."

"Ranger, you have a way of distancing yourself from people. I bet that no one ever gets to really know you and that if they get too close, you have a way of pushing them away. Dan, I like you, and I don't want to be one of those people you push away. I believe that I am what you need and that you are what I need right now. It could change in the future, but I hope not."

"What do you have to say about that?"

"Sonia, I like you. That is hard for me to admit, and I don't think I'll be pushing you away. We have arrived at Clancy's, and I want to show you a good time. It has been said that I am difficult to know and that I am not quite human. I have a fierce temper that can be all consuming when I get angry. But don't pay much attention to that."

"Good evening, madam and sir. I am Sean. Do you have reservations?"

"Yes and the name is Dan Mesa.""May I seat you?"

"Yes, please. If possible, may we have a table that isn't too far from the dance floor?"

"Sir, I believe this table will be to your liking."

"Thank you, Sean."

"Your waiter will be over shortly with our wine list. What can I get you from the bar?"

I ask Sonia what she would like.

"I'd like an Amaretto sour, and a cherry, please," she answers.

"I am impressed. That is my favorite drink. I will have the same, please."

I developed a liking for Amaretto sometime back. It has a most pleasing taste and aroma. I also use Amaretto-flavored creamer.

"Dan, how did you wind up here in Arizona after such a colorful life? You seem to have seen and done a lot of things. It seems so odd that you are here."

"I have always wanted to live in either Arizona or New Mexico. I am a person who enjoys the desert and the quiet. I am a loner for the most part, and the desert contributes to the lonely life. I was looking for a job and someone mentioned the Rangers. I have always been aware of the Rangers. When I was a child there was a TV western called *The Twenty-Six Men.* It was the story of the Arizona Rangers. So just by chance there was an opening in the Rangers and I got the job. I have been a Ranger since retiring in 1994. It was and is a blessing for me. It literally saved my life after my wife left me. I was a broken man and needed somewhere to belong, and the Rangers were the answer. I can't think of a better group of men and women to work with. I am not the average person of this area, I admit. My last name is a Spanish surname. Mesa is our family name; we're French Creole, which is French, Spanish, Native American, and black. My family took the Spanish name, thus Mesa. We are also one of the black Indian tribes of Oklahoma. My grandfather moved to Wewoka, Oklahoma, in the early 1900s. So as you can see, I have an interesting family tree."

"Ranger Mesa, you are an interesting person."

"Sir, may I take your orders?"

"Yes, thank you. Sonia, if you please?"

"Thanks. I'll have the trout amandine, with green beans, scalloped potatoes, and a salad," she says.

"I'll have the grilled salmon, with green beans, rice, and a salad also."

"Thank you, madam and sir. I'll turn your order in and bring the salads."

Our drinks are here. "Dan, you should ask me to dance," Sonia says.

"My lady, I do apologize for my unintended transgression." The band is playing Lou Rawls's "Lady Love."

"Sonia, I'm going to leave on Monday for Yuma, trailing Jackson, and I don't know when I'll return. I never know if I'll return. It is something I have lived with for a long time. If you decide you want to be a part of my life, you will have to accept it also.""Dan, I know what kind of life you lead. Remember, I was married to a policeman, and I suffered through his death. I'll admit to you, the idea frightens me a lot. Oh, the song has ended. Please, dance with me for another song." I love this one—"Crazy," by Patsy Cline.

"Lady, you are an amazing dancer. I haven't enjoyed dancing like this in a long time. I may never go home. Ah, our food is arriving."

"How is your trout and is it what you ordered?"

"Yes, it is quite good."

We finish dinner and are headed outside when Sonia answers.

"Dan, I have really had a great time. Dan, what is that guy doing over there?"

"Duck, Sonia, and stay here no matter what happens!"

Mesa moves quickly to his right away from the light and into the shasows. In a loud voice he says, "Mister, drop that gun and step away from the lady. I won't tell you again. I don't want to kill you, but I will if you don't drop that gun right now. The gunman reaches for his gun. Mesa draws his weapon with lighting speed and fires as his gun comes to a level position.

In a split second Ranger Mesa kills his second man in less than two days, a fact not lost on Sonia.

Mesa walks carefully towards the woman lying on the ground he says, "Lady, I know you're not dead, so get up slow. If you're carrying a gun, you'd best drop it now."

She replies, "Please, Ranger, don't shoot! I'm getting up! Just don't shoot!"

Mesa checks the man for a pulse while keeping he eyes on the lady. The man is dead, so Mesa cuffs the lady and waits for the police to arrive.

A crowd has gathered and the police are arriving.

As the police arrive Mesa identifies himselve saying, "Officers, I am Ranger Mesa of the Santa Cruz Company, and I believe the lady and the gentleman lying there were sent to kill me. He tried but wasn't up to it. She decided she wanted to live little longer surrendered. It is the second attempt on my life in two days."

"Well, Ranger, he won't be shooting at anyone else. We'll take her in to custody, and you can follow us in and make a report."

Oh my God! Where is Sonia?"Sonia, are you okay? I am so sorry about this. If I had known this was going to happen, I would never have asked you out. We have to go by the police station and make a report. Are you sure you are okay?"

"Just finish this up and take me home! This I don't need. Dan, you just shot a man and you're as calm as can be. Doesn't anything shake you?"

"Sonia, please calm down and take it easy. What would you have me do, let that guy kill me? I don't think so!"

"Officer, I'm Ranger Dan Mesa, and I was involved in a shooting at Clancy's Restaurant. I'm here to make a written report. I have a lady friend with me who saw the shooting and she's a bit upset. I would appreciate it if you would allow her to stay with me while I write the report."

As Mesa writes his report, shift Captain Mendoza walks in and says, "I am Captain Mendoza. Can you tell me how all this got started?"

"Captain I was having dinner with my friend at Clancy's and when we finished dinner and walked outside, she noticed the man and lady and they were pointing at me. I challenged them and he went for his gun. He wasn't as fast as he thought he was. I killed him and she surrendered."

"Captain Mendosa, will you please call my captain, Captain Johnson, and explain to him what happened? I may be in trouble."

"Sure. I know JohnsonHe is a good man. Mesa, are you okay? That was some quick action out there. You are lucky to be alive. That guy you shot is a professional. We have a flier on him, and he's world class when it comes to shooting people."

"Yes, sir, I'm fine. I know who hired him to kill me. It was José Gutierrez-Jackson, a man wanted for murder and robbery who was once my best friend."

"Ranger, you should choose your friends more carefully. All right, take your lady friend home and keep a close look out. I don't believe this is the end."

"Sonia, we have arrived at your place. Again, I am sorry this hap—"

"Ranger, I am tired and I am going in. I'll talk to you some other time."

Well, I guess I've messed up this relationship before it even got started. I didn't want to shoot that fellow, but he didn't give me much of a choice. I'm not sure what else I could have done.

I am home now. Someone has tried to kill me twice, and I am slowly getting a little angry.

"Captain Johnson, Mesa here. Sir, I guess you've heard what happened."

"Yes, Dan, I heard it from Mendoza. Are you and the lady okay?"

"Yes, sir, we are both okay, although I believe I lost something tonight I really wanted. Captain, she is angry with me because I shot that fellow. What was I supposed to do?"

"Sergeant, you ask questions for which there aren't any easy answers. Just try talking to her but give her some time. What are you going to do about these attempts on your life? You and I know who is responsible.""Yes, I know. I will be in to work tomorrow. I've reached the conclusion that Jackson is not my friend anymore. He's bent on my destruction, and that isn't going to happen. Now I'm angry, and that isn't good for Jackson. I will make him pay for his transgressions."

Well, it is time for bed. Tomorrow is another day, and I have a lot to do.

It seems as if I just closed my eyes and now it is morning and I have to face the Captain. It feels as though I am always on the defense. Well I'm at Headquarters and now to see the Captain.

"Sergeant Mesa, when you finish signing in, come to my office."

"Yes, sir, I am on my way."

I finish my report and walk towards the Captain's office with some apprehension. I knock before entering saying, "Captain you want to see me?"

"Come in, Dan. How are you this morning, and how is Sonia?"

"I am adjusting, sir. As for Sonia, I haven't spoken to her since last night. I got the feeling she doesn't want to see me again."

"Well, all you can do is wait and hope she'll get over it. Sometimes they do and sometimes they don't. As I recall, she was married to a policeman who was killed in the line of duty, right?"

"Yes, sir, he was, and I guess what happened last night brought back bad memories. But sir, why did she have to blame me for what happened?"

"I don't know, Dan, and maybe she doesn't either. Anyway, let's talk about what happened. Do you have any ideas about who is trying to kill you?"

"Sir, I believe Jackson or some of his relatives have put a contract on me and someone is trying to collect on it. According to Captain Mendoza, the guy I shot is a professional killer. Someone with money hired that fellow, and to be honest, sir, I am madder than a scalded snake about it and ready to make someone pay."

"Sergeant, I know you and I know that temper of yours. Don't do anything you'll regret, and remember, you wear a badge. That badge stands for a lot, and I know how much it means to you, so remember that."

"I know you are right, Captain, but when someone tries to kill me, I take it personally. They—whoever they are—have tried twice, and I don't plan on there being a third time. I do respect this badge and I will not disgrace it, I promise."

"Okay, Dan. What do you plan to do now?"

"Captain, Jackson has a host of family and friends in Yuma and I suspect he has gone there. As you may recall, we had a run-in with some of his friends at Los Negritos. They said he had changed vehicles and was headed toward Yuma. Sir, once he gets to Yuma, his family will protect him and we'll have a tough time taking him. I believe he has already gone there. I suggest we contact the Yuma police and acquaint them with the situation and let them know we'll be heading into their area."

"Sergeant, I am sending you to Yuma to investigate. If you need help, just call and we'll come running. Don't—I repeat, don't—get yourself killed. I don't want to have to explain to the lady why I got you killed, okay?"

"I will do my best to stay alive, sir, and I'll see you when I see you."

Somewhere in Yuma, Arizona, another scenario is opening involving Jackson.

"José, it's good to see you, man. I hear you've had some trouble in Nogales and that one of the Rangers is on your trail. Which one is it?"

"Benito, it's Daniel Mesa, and I do believe I've screwed up royally. I shot at him in his house on Friday night and hired a hit man to take him out on Saturday night at Clancy's. But Mesa took him out. Dan is no fool. He probably knows I hired the hit man, and he'll come looking for me. I know him well. We were best friends a long time back, but those days are gone now. He will kill me if he gets the chance."

"Partner, it seems as if we need to put together a plan, some kind of welcoming committee for Ranger Mesa. We can call the cousins together, and that should do the job. Miguel and Jaime are like caged tigers that smell blood. Martha is just as bloodthirsty as the boys."

"Hello, Momma, I'm afraid I'm bringing trouble to your home. Dan Mesa is after me, and this time, he smells blood."

"What have you done, son? I've heard of this Señor Mesa. It is said he is part Indio and a very sad man. I fear there will be much trouble for this family. José, you have been a very bad boy."

"Momma, I have done some bad things, but I will not go back to prison, not even for Daniel Mesa. I do regret getting him involved in this whole thing. To make things worse I tried to have him killed. Dan doesn't ever forget or forgive. I will have to kill him or he will kill me."

"Son, we will protect you as much as possible, but I will have no part in killing a Ranger. I tell you now, do not bring him to this house dead or alive."

"Benito, do you have any friends on the police force who can keep us informed of what is going on there? The Rangers will contact the Yuma police and let them know about me."

"Yeah, I know a couple of guys on the force, but I can't guarantee they'll do it. I'll ask, though."

"Momma, I don't know how this is going to end, but I won't die without taking someone with me. I hope it won't be Dan. We were the best of friends at one time. He always treated me right. I guess somewhere along the way something happened and that friendship got pushed aside. That is one thing I regret. I also regret taking a contract out on him, but not enough to let him take me in. I won't go back to prison."

"Son, I love you, but don't start the fight here. Take it someplace away from here. I won't have my home turned into a war zone. I won't put your father and myself at risk, so you can't stay here. I recommend going to the place north of here."

"Captain Johnson, Colonel Grant here. I got your report on the latest on Jackson and have instructed the Yuma group to give Mesa whatever he needs to capture him. Sam, is Mesa in over his head?"

"Colonel, Sergeant Mesa is damn good at this kind of search-and-destroy tactic, and Jackson used to be his best friend. Now that best friend has put a contract on Mesa that has caused Dan to be furious and a little prone to excessive brutality, but I talked with him, and he gave me his word he would follow procedure. Once Dan gives his word to you, he'll keep it."

"Okay, Captain, keep me informed about how this is progressing. I don't want a lot of civilians hurt or killed. The Rangers have a good rapport with the civilians, so let's keep it that way. Take care."

Captain Johnson walks to the door and say; "Sergeant Mendoza, call Sergeant Mesa and tell him I am sending Ranger Savalas with him and no arguments about it."

"Mrs. Gutierrez-Jackson, I am Major Stein of the Arizona State Police. The reason I'm calling is to tell you that your son José is in trouble with the law and it is to his advantage to turn himself in. If he does, I can promise him it will have considerable influence when he goes to trial. Other than that I can't make any promises. His crimes are serious, involving armed robbery, the murder of a police officer, and the attempted murder of two others: the marshal of Patagonia and the attempted contract murder of Ranger Daniel Mesa. He has until midnight tonight to turn himself in. One minute after twelve he is a wanted fugitive with a fifty-thousand-dollar reward for his capture, dead or alive. As you can see the reward has increased substantially."

"Señor Stein, I will tell him, but that is all I can or will do. He is my son and I will not turn him in, nor will any member of this family. If he decides, it will be on his own. It is his life. I am sorry, señor." She puts the phone down and turns toward Benito.

"Benito, tell your brother it is time to leave and head into the higher country, as the police will be hunting him as of midnight tonight. Also—oh, there you are, José. There is a fifty-thousand-dollar reward for your capture, dead or alive. As of midnight tonight you are a fugitive from justice, according to a Major Stein of the state police. He said you have the option of turning yourself in and that it will be considered at your trial. My son, you are wanted for the murder of four policemen and the attempted murder of murder of your friend Daniel Mesa, the Ranger. José, you have been a bad son and you will have to make amends. You must leave now!"

"Momma, I am sorry to cause you so much grief. I will leave as you have requested. Poppa, you have always been good to me. I guess I just never appreciated it before. I will go now."

"*Via con Dios,* my son."

"Benito, get Carlos, Miguel, Sammy, and Jaime. Tell them to come armed for war. This will not be an easy task. Some of us will not return, so make sure you tell them that. Let's go now and we'll meet at the cabin. I am sure someone is watching us right now."

"Dan, what is our plan of action once we get to Yuma?"

Savalas asks; "How do we find Jackson?"

"We'll check in with the Rangers there and the local police. The captain has already notified the Rangers and the state police that we are coming. I'm sure they've already begun actions to apprehend Jackson. I will tell you this, some of us will not return from this siege. When it hits the fan, you make sure you have your vest on.

I have seen enough policemen get killed these last few days, and I don't want any more casualties."

"Dan, do you believe Jackson will try to fight us? You were his best friend at one time. Will he shoot at you?"

"Savalas, Jackson is a desperate man and will do whatever is necessary to survive, even to the point of killing me and anyone who gets in his way. Yes, we were friends, but that was in another time. Today he is just another criminal who is trying to evade capture. I will shoot him the same as I would a rabid dog. Twice he has tried to kill me or have me killed. He is no longer a friend of mine."

"Dan, I would hate to get on your bad side, because you'd make a terrible foe. People like you are difficult to know and understand. You live by a code that is as old as time itself yet very useful."

"I know the things I believe in are somewhat old-fashioned, but I say to you they will live on. I know I am the last of a breed of people who are dying out. When I am dead and gone, I will be lucky if anyone ever remembers I lived, and few will remember what we did as Rangers.

"Sometimes I get carried away when I get on the subject of right and wrong. Some people have a very low opinion of what is right. I have to believe in right and wrong because it is what I live by. As a Ranger, I am expected to be in compliance with the law."

I have this premonition about this trip to Yuma. I know it will turn out badly for all concerned. Now what do I do about Sonia? It seems as if all my relationships turn out bad.

There goes the phone. "Mesa here. Hello Captain. "Dan, the Yuma police called and reported that José is there at his mother's place. The state police seem to believe that Jackson and his family are expecting you. It seems there were a lot of cars and trucks parked at the house.

The State Police have good reason to know about José. Apparently he cut a wide trail through Yuma during his youth. It is apparent he hasn't changed. Sergeant, be careful around José, because as you know, he isn't the same person he used to be. He is a killer! Check in with the Rangers when you get to Yuma and also check in with the police. Major McMasters is the commander of the Rangers in Yuma, and he is a great guy. Dan, on a personal note Sonia called to check on you and to make sure you were okay. Is there anything you want me to tell her? If so let me know. She seemed to be quite concerned about you."

"No, sir, there isn't anything I want you to tell her. I have to concentrate on catching José. But thanks for caring, sir."

Savalas is looking at me as if I am crazy. I know what is coming next.

"Mesa, are you crazy? That lady is great looking and seems to have a lot of class, and obviously she cares about you. So can you please tell me why you need to be so difficult?"

"I know, but I can't afford to occupy my mind with frivolous thoughts, and right now thinking of her would cause me to not be totally focused on what I need to do. Someone is going to die before this is over, and I don't plan on it being me."

We have finally arrived in Yuma. I find that my mind is on Sonia, which is not good. I guess I need to check in with Major McMasters.

"Hi, I'm Sergeant Mesa from the Santa Cruz Company and I'm supposed to check in with Major McMasters about José Gutierrez-Jackson."

"Sergeant, I'm Lieutenant Alana Osborne. Welcome to Yuma. The major is off today, but we are aware of the Jackson problem, believe me! We have been watching his mother's house and a lot of people have been going in and out. It appears they are getting ready for a war. Also, our spies tell us the sons have gone into the hills behind their ranch. That will require horses, because the terrain out there is rocky and full of cactus and rattlers. There are several places to ambush us when we start climbing. I have also notified the state police and the Sheriff's office."

"Ma'am, it appears you covered everything. I know the family well, and yes, they will be a force to deal with. We cannot take them for granted. There are several of them, and they are all difficult people to reason with. Also they are very clannish. Ma'am, please issue all your people body armor. I don't mean to appear overly cautious, but I know them quite well, and I know what José is capable of doing. I don't believe we'll come out of this without someone dying or being seriously hurt."

"Sergeant Mesa, may I ask you a question?"

"Yes, you may."

"I was told that you and Jackson were friends or had been friends at one time. If that is true, what happened to turn him into the killer that he has become?"

"Well, after we left college—or I should say after I finished college and joined the air force—I lost touch with José for a while. He dropped out of college and joined the Peace Corps and spent time in South America and Africa. I didn't see him again until 1978, when I returned to the States from England. I was assigned to Albuquerque at Kirtland Air Force Base, and I got in touch with his mom and she got in touch with him. He was living in El Paso at the time, so we became close again—almost like brothers. We both liked the border towns, so we spent a lot of our free time on the border. We were a force to be reckoned with."

"Okay, but what changed him?"

"I guess he never grew up, plus he started hanging around with some people of unsavory character. The next thing I heard was that he had killed a fellow in Mexico over a girl. Then there was an incident in San Antonio where there were accusations of him being involved in an armed robbery. I tried talking to him, but he refused to listen so I had to cut him loose. After that he became very wild and would do anything on a dare. He spent two years in jail for a crime he didn't commit and that sent him over the edge. The robbery of the armored truck and the killing of the two guards just pushed him farther. edge.The phone rings and she answers it. She calls me to the phone.

"Sergeant, it's for you."

"Mesa here."

"Dan, this is José. I knew they would send you after me. Dan, go home. I don't want to kill you. We have been friends a long time, and I don't want to fight you, but I am not going back to jail."

"José, when you killed those two guards and stole the money, you gave me no alternative. Since then you have killed two police officers and tried to kill me twice. I am the victim here. Someone has to stop you, and the job has fallen to me. I regret having to do it, but you have left us no other choice. I hoped you'd give yourself up. Now it is too late, because I'm coming for you and anyone who gets in my way."

"Then, Ranger, prepare to kill or be killed. I will not hold back just because we used to be friends."

"Lieutenant, that was Jackson. He knows we are going after him. I must go and prepare for this trip, but first I'll get a bite to eat. Savalas, are you hungry?"

"Dan, I am going to hang around and visit here for a while. I'll see you later."

"Ranger Savalas, tell me about Ranger Mesa. He seems to be a puzzle."

"Ma'am, I've known him for only two years. He joined the Rangers in 1995 after retiring from the air force. He immediately achieved a reputation as a fair and honest man but a hard one. He doesn't give one inch when it comes to the law. He was married, but she left him and took the boy and moved back east. That almost destroyed him. He loved her and that boy dearly. After she left, he almost lost it. He drank a lot, and it was through sheer animal toughness and a good friend that he made it through without losing everything. Now he is just iron tough and doesn't let anyone get too close. I guess that is his way of dealing with life now."

"When did his wife leave?"

"I heard she left back in '96 and hasn't been back. There was a lady in Amado, but I guess that is over. On Saturday last, they were in Tucson at Clancy's and an agent hired by Jackson tried to kill Dan and failed. Dan shot and killed him. The lady was standing there and she fell apart and blamed Dan or something to that effect. Anyway, it hurt Dan because I believe he liked her a lot. It was the first time I have seen him interested in anyone other than the wife who left."

"Lieutenant, it's none of my business, but if you are getting interested in Sergeant Mesa, you could be in for some hard times. Dan is a good man but harder than nails and mean as a scalded snake when he gets angry. Last week I saw him take out a fellow when we raided a bar in Nogales and he never broke a sweat. He is getting meaner every day. He does need someone, but she'll have to be a strong woman, and she'll have to be prepared to try to get beyond that hard exterior. This thing with Jackson is going hard with him because he and Jackson were like brothers. Dan will have to kill Jackson, and that will be hard on him."

"Why did he accept this assignment?"

"It was given to him because no one else can do what he can. Captain Johnson initially thought that maybe Jackson would give himself up because of Dan."

"Ma'am, Sergeant Mesa served in Vietnam, and it is rumored that he had to kill some people there. He also served in the Gulf War, and he was almost killed twice by terrorists. I know since he has been a Ranger he has killed at least three people, all in the line of duty while saving someone else's life. He lives by a set of rules that are outdated by today's society, but they do make a lot of sense. He is the last of a breed."

Sometimes I think maybe it is time to call it quits as a Ranger, but then what would I do? I know I have many skills and can do many things, but there are few I enjoy as much as being a Ranger. In another year I will complete my doctorate in psychology, and I can always hang my shingle up. I see an Applebee's and they have a decent salad. "Welcome to Applebee's."

"May I have the grilled veggies with rice and iced tea, please?"

"Excuse me, Ranger, but could you assist us? We have a gentleman who refuses to pay his bill and is threatening the manager."

"Okay, lead on."

"What seems to be the problem here?"

There is always someone who thinks he is ten feet tall and bulletproof. This fellow has a serious problem with life.

"So, they sent for the big gun. I will tell you the same thing I told them. I am not going to pay for this food because it took too long for the waiter to bring it."

"Sir, if that was the case, why didn't you just leave before they brought the food to you? It is apparent that you took the time to eat it. Now you must pay for it or it's called stealing."

"Well, they should have brought it sooner, because I am not paying for it."

"Sir, you don't have a choice. Pay now or pay later, it's up to you."

The gent throws a punch at me, and I respond with a solid right to the chest and a hop-kido kick to the stomach.

"Ma'am, call the police and tell them to send a squad car to this location."

"Sergeant Mesa, can't you go to lunch without getting into trouble?"

"Lieutenant, it does seem that I am always in the right place at the wrong time.I was going to have lunch, but I'll wait until later. Ma'am, what is the latest on Jackson?"

"The sheriff hasn't called in yet and neither have the state police. We are in a wait-and-see mode."

At the Gutierrez-Jackson homestead, the family and friends of José are preparing a welcome for the Rangers.

Benito speaks saying; "José, you do realize that if a Ranger is killed, or any law officer is killed, this entire family will be pursued until all of us are dead or apprehended. I have a feeling we will pay a big price for our actions. Are you sure you want to put your parents through this?"

"Benito, I will not go to jail again. So if you want out, say so now. Once this thing starts, there isn't any turning back. You will be committed. As for Mom and Pop, I am sending them away from here."

"Mom, you and Dad will have to leave this area and not return until the siege is over. Go to the police station and tell them I sent you away and that I am waiting for them and the Rangers, especially Dan Mesa!"

"Son, this whole affair is going to end badly for you. If you kill Mesa, you will die here or they will follow you to hell and back. You can't win."

"Pop, I know, but I will not go back to prison ever again."

Benito with a sad expression says: "José, I am leaving with your Mom and Dad. I will not be a party to ambushing the police. It is wrong and I don't want any part of it."

"Jaime, what are your feelings on the matter?"

"You are my brother and I will follow you, plus I have a bone to pick with Ranger Mesa and the police."

"Okay, Mom and Dad have gone away, so it's time to set the trap. First, set charges along the trail with these old Claymore mines. Set that old tree across the road and put another mine behind it. Take that other tree and put it farther up the hill. Brace it in place so that it takes only a little push to come tumbling down. It may not stop them, but it surely will make them cautious."

"José, you are psychotic, but I like it."

"Martha, you have arrived. Who do you think of our little party?"

43

" "Hey, where is Benito?"

"Benito decided he wanted out. Maybe he is better off."

"I am disappointed in him. I thought he'd stand with us. It looks like you have prepared well. Where do you want me to take up a position?"

"Martha, are you sure you want to be a part of this?"

"Yes I am, so don't start treating me like some girl!"

"Okay. Move up the hill behind that second log. It is a booby trap, so be careful. If they make it this far, push on that log and run like hell!"

"José, what happens if all this doesn't work? You know Mesa will never give up as long as you are alive. You tried to kill him and then you hired someone for the job and neither one of you succeeded. If I were Dan, I'd nail your hide to the door. You should have hired a woman for the job. He'd be dead."

"Martha, if this goes badly, go straight to Mexico and don't come back for a while. Dan knows all of the cousins and will be looking for all of you. If I fail here, then Dan and I will have to face each other, and I am not so sure I can win."

"Then why do all this stuff when you could be in Mexico yourself? I don't see the sense in any of this if you know you can't win."

"It's simple: I don't want to live in Mexico. I like it here and I am not going to Mexico and I am not going back to prison, so I will stay here and live or die."

It is amazing how things work out in life. I have myself a predicament. Can I really kill a man whom I called my brother at one time? It has been said of me that I am a capable person with few feelings if any. Well, only time will tell.

"Lieutenant, what is the latest from the state police and city police?"

"They haven't called yet and we can't move until they do. So, you might as well get comfortable and prepare to wait while Jackson and his group prepare a trap for us."

"Sergeant Mesa, what will you do when this is over?"

"Ma'am, I should take a vacation, but who knows.""You know, we have some nice areas for camping and getting away from everything. I like the Four Corners area where the cliff dwellings are."

"Yes, ma'am, I like that area myself. I have spent some time exploring that area, and I plan to go back before too long. I really like that area. You know, sometimes it feels as if I lived during that time. I know it sounds crazy, but then, maybe I am."

"Sergeant, you are welcome at my campfire any day. Why don't you join me in August when I go?"

Now what do I say to this? I don't want to make promises I can't keep.

"Lieutenant, I would like that, but I'll have to check and see if I can get the time off."

"Sergeant, why are you a Ranger? You have the credentials to be anything you want. So why a Ranger?"

"I don't know, really, except it involves being my own man and enjoying the job. I really like what I do. Sure, I could make more money doing something else, but I wouldn't be nearly as happy. I guess I am meant to be what I am. I am good at what I do. I was an excellent teacher also and could go back to teaching, but I don't like being shut up in a classroom teaching high school kids. If I could find another position teaching college, I would be very happy—or should I say, I would have been happy, but that was in another world and too many bad memories ago."

"Well, it is apparent we aren't going to get anything done today. It's almost 1800 hours and definitely too late to make any kind of assault on Jackson's hideout now. Listen up, everyone: it is Sunday evening and tomorrow is going to be a rough day, so go home and be back here at 0600 hours tomorrow. Come prepared to stay out for a few days. Tell your families what you are doing and where you will be. They may not see you for at least a week. "Sergeant, what are your plans for this evening?"

"I haven't got any, although I need to find a room for Savalas and myself."

Savalas smiles and says; "Dan, I am going to visit my uncle and aunt and spend the night with them, so you are on your own. I will see you tomorrow at 0600."

"Mesa, why don't you let Savalas take your truck and I will drop you off at the Marriott or wherever you'd like to stay?"

"That is a good idea. Okay, take the truck and we will meet here tomorrow."

The Lieutenant smiles and says;"My truck is parked in the back. I just bought it, and man, do I like it. It's a Dodge extended cab with four-wheel drive and a manual transmission, black and red with leather seats. I have always wanted one, and I finally persuaded myself to buy one. I traded in my Nissan Pathfinder, which I purchased new in '92. I had more than two hundred thousand miles on it.

"Dan, do you mind if I call you Dan?"

"No, ma'am, that is my name."

"The Marriott is probably the best place to stay, and law enforcement types get a discount there. So if it is okay with you, I'll take you by there and get you settled in."

"That sounds like a good plan."

"Hello, Cynthia, this is Ranger Mesa from Nogales, and he's working with us for few days. Do you have a room for him?"

"Yes, how about Room 229? It is up the elevator to the second floor and to your left."

"Alana, isn't he that gunslinging Ranger from Nogales who shot that fellow a couple of days ago and then another one on Saturday night?"

"Cynthia, he is not a gunslinger, and yes to both."

"Alana, don't get testy. One would think you like him."

"Oh, go and find some work to do!"

Alana thinks to herself, "Oh my goodness, do I have a crush on this guy? Surely not. He is so serious and sad and doesn't ever smile."

"Lieutenant, I thank you for your help. If you could recommend a good restaurant, I'd be grateful."

"Well, I am a fair cook and my mom is an excellent cook, and I would appreciate the company, because my mother is a handful but a delightful person to be around. So I guess what I am doing is inviting you to dinner at my house if you'd like to come."

"Well, I guess it is okay. Are you sure I won't be intruding?"

"No, you won't be, and I know Mom will enjoy meeting you. My father was a Texas Ranger until his death about ten years ago. He was a real Texas hero. I guess that is why I'm an Arizona Ranger."

"If you don't mind my asking, was he killed in the line of duty?"

"Yes, he was. He was the one who captured the Mitchell Trio. Do you remember them? They were the ones who stole the three armored cars loaded with money and disappeared for two years. He tracked them for two years and captured them in Muleshoe, Texas. He was killed a year later while responding to a robbery in El Paso."

"I am sorry about your loss. I know it must have been hard on you and your mother.""Yes, it was hard on her for a while. She and Dad were like teenagers and were in love to the end. He brought her a flower every day of their marriage. He was my father but he was more. He was the best friend I have ever had. Now Mom and I are really close—more like sisters than anything, and she is absolutely a pleasure to be around. I promise you will like her."

"Lieutenant, most people don't take to me too easily. So don't be surprised if she doesn't like me."

"We are at my house now."

"My goodness, what did you father do other than be a Ranger? This house is easily worth a half million dollars or more."

"It's not worth that much, but it is a really nice place. Dad bought this land in the early fifties and basically built the house himself with help from a few friends. We have about fifty acres in this area and another ten across the road."

"Ma'am, it is apparent that you are a lady of some wealth. I come from poor stock that never owned anything. I have had to fight for everything I have, but I am proud of who I am and what I have accomplished."

These people are over my head. I can't match up. I couldn't imagine living in a house like this. I like her, but there is unfinished business with Sonia. How do I handle it if she is interested in me?

"Dan, I never measure a person by the money they have or the things they have. I measure people by their sincerity and what is in their heart. I couldn't care less if a man is rich. What I care about is his sincerity and how much he loves and respects my family and me. He would have to get along with Mom in order for me to get along with him."

"Ma'am, you appear to be an amazing lady."

"My dear sir, what do you mean by saying I appear to be an amazing lady? Either I am or I am not an amazing lady."

"Lieutenant, I don't know you well enough to say whether you're being truthful. However, I prefer to believe you are being truthful. I am not a trusting person. I have put my trust in people who have proven to be less than what I expected. It makes me somewhat suspect of everyone."

"Ranger, you are saved by the bell. This is my mom, Adelaide Matilda Osborne. Mom, may I introduce Sergeant Daniel Mesa, of the Santa Cruz Company of the Arizona Rangers."

"Mrs. Osborne, it is my pleasure to meet you, ma'am. You have a most interesting daughter."

"It is a pleasure to meet you, Mr. Mesa, and welcome to our home."

"Thank you, ma'am. If you don't mind, would you please call me Dan? I am just an ordinary guy."

49

"Okay, Dan it is. Alana, I like this fellow!"

"Okay, Mommy, no match making tonight."

"Then turning to me, she says, "She believes I need to be married.""

"Dan, you have a choice of grilled steak or trout, with sweet potatoes and grilled vegetables. For dessert we have apple pie and pecan pie."

"Ma'am, I usually eat fish, but if it is okay with you, I'd like a steak since I haven't had one in some time. I have been trying to eat more healthfully."

"Mom, I'd like a steak also, please."

"Dan, make yourself handy and put these steaks on the grill. They have been seasoned—all you have to do is watch them. I like mine well done but not burned and so does Alana."

"I like mine well done also. Mrs. Osborne, this place is really nice. How many head of horses do you have?"

"We have about fifty head of horses and about twenty-five head of cows. We also have two mules, four burros, and a pond full of fish. I like to ride, and I still fish. Do you ride?"

"Yes, ma'am, I ride. I used to be a professional cowboy. I gave it up when I joined the air force but still ride as often as I can. I own an Appaloosa mix and she is ten years old. I try to ride her at least twice a week, but the last two weeks have been very difficult."

"So tell me, what brings you to Yuma?"

"I've been tracking a fellow by the name of José Gutierrez-Jackson, who is wanted for murder and armed robbery. I have trailed him to his parents' house, and I'm now working with the Rangers here to capture him."

"Now I know who you are! You're that Ranger who killed the fellow in Nogales, and another in Tucson on Saturday night. The paper said the fellow was hired to kill you. Is that true?"

"Yes, he was paid by Jackson to shoot me, but I was somewhat faster than he was. A lady friend was with me and saw the shooting. Now she refuses to talk to me."

"The steaks are ready if you ladies are ready. If I do say so myself, they look great. There isn't anything like the smell of steak." Alana thinks to herself, "I wonder what Mom thinks of Dan. He is so nice and respectful. He has a look about him that worries me. There is something about him that tells you not to get too close. I believe I really like him, so what do I do now? A lady can't be too careful. I remember what Savalas said about the lady in Nogales."

"How is the steak?"

"Ma'am, mine is great, and the sweet potatoes have a cinnamon taste to them—something I like."

"Dan, you are welcome here any time you are in Yuma. As a matter of fact you should come by more often and ride some of these horses. I don't ride anymore, and Alana can never ride all of them."

"Well, thank you, ma'am, I may take you up on the offer. It is nice here and you do have a large area for riding."

"Dan, would you care for coffee and dessert?"

"Yes, thank you. It is nice to eat something someone else cooked. I am not much of a cook. My cooking is so bad the dog won't eat it."

"It sounds like you need a wife!"

"Mom, don't you dare start matchmaking again. Dan, she is always trying to marry me off. She believes I'm going to be an old maid."

"No, I don't, I just want my daughter to be happy and for me to have grandchildren before I am too old. Have you ever been married?"

"Yes, ma'am, it appears I goofed up."

"Okay, enough of this. It is time for coffee and dessert."

"Alana what are your chances of capturing Jackson without having to kill him?"

"Mom, you'll have to ask Sergeant Mesa about that. He knows Jackson quite well and has been chasing him for a while."

"Mrs. Osborne, Jackson has gone too far, and he knows that the murder of a police officer is a federal crime. Also, he has murdered four officers of the law and is staring the death penalty in the face. So, he has nothing to lose. We will have to take him out personally, and that is something I will regret. I don't like killing, but sometimes it is unavoidable."

"Dan, do you ever worry about the possibility of getting shot yourself?"

"No, ma'am, I have been shot twice and it doesn't worry me anymore. I try to be as careful as possible and use good common sense. I know I am not ten feet tall and bulletproof. I also know that I could be killed crossing the street, so I put it in God's hands."

"Jim, my husband, was like you in some ways. He loved being a Texas Ranger and was proud to wear the star. I was just as proud of him. It took a lot to get through the rough times after his death. I thought I would lose my mind, but Jim always said, 'Keep looking for the silver lining,' and that is what I did. Alana is my silver lining. Sometimes it is as if we are more like friends than like mother and daughter. Maybe it is because I had her at a young age. I was twenty when she was born, and now I am fifty-eight. If Jim were alive, he would be sixty now. I still miss him a lot."

"Mom and I do everything together. I am actively looking for a boyfriend for her. Ranger, you are about the right age."

"Alana Osborne, what do you think you are doing?"

"Oh, Mom, he is a nice guy, and you need to get out more. Dan, she hasn't been on a date since Dad's death. I know he would want her to get out and enjoy life. He was an ideal man and the best husband and father that ever lived. He always found time to bring Mom flowers and me something even after I was a grown woman. He visited the sick and helped everyone. I hope I can be half the person he was."

"He will be a hard act to follow. I have known men like that in my life, and they always leave a void when they are gone. I should be so fortunate."

"Okay, Dan, how about some more coffee?"

"Well, another cup and then I had better get back and get ready for tomorrow."

"Ranger, what do you expect to happen tomorrow?"

"I never anticipate. I go prepared for everything and keep an open mind and a keen eye. I know that some of us will not return when this is over. It will not end tomorrow. Jackson will not be that easy to capture. Thanks for the dinner. Ma'am, it has been a while since I enjoyed anything similar to this. I thank both of you. You look more like sisters than mother and daughter. A man would be most fortunate to have either one of you to care about him."

"Dan Mesa, you are a gentleman and a scholar, and I do mean both. You are welcome at this house anytime."

"Lieutenant, may I bum a ride back to my motel and I thank you for inviting me to your house. I really enjoyed myself. A man would be fortunate to have you or your mom to care for."

"So which one of us do you like?"

"I like both of you the same. I can't decide. I never thought I would meet anyone like the two of you. You are absolutely beautiful, and you mom is just a more mature version of you. Your father was a most fortunate man. I would be less than a man to come between the two of you. I think I will just love you both as my best friends for now and maybe one day things will change. For now just accept me as a very dear friend."

"Ranger, we will work on you later, but for now you are a very dear friend. So good night, and I will see you tomorrow."

Dan Mesa, you are a most fortunate person also. You met two really great people in one day.

"Good evening, Ranger. I hope you had a good evening with Alana and her mom. They are two of the nicest people in Yuma."

"Ma'am, I agree with you one hundred percent. I will say good night. I'll see you tomorrow."

It is time for bed because tomorrow will be a rough day. Oops, there goes the phone.

"Dan, this is Savalas. I am just checking to see if there's anything new for tomorrow."

"No, but make sure you are wearing your body armor tomorrow. Don't take any chances, and remember they will be shooting to kill. I will see you tomorrow morning at six o'clock."

I wonder what Sonia is doing. I would call her, but it is best to just leave things as they are. Man, I sure do have a knack for destroying relationships. If it is meant to be, it will be.

Daylight surely does come quick. A shower and a shave and then breakfast.

The Lieutenant should be in by now.

"Good morning, Sergeant Mesa. Are you ready for today's activity?"

"Ma'am, I am ready but not happy about it. This is not going to be an easy pursuit. I know Jackson and his family, and they are a force to reckon with. Ma'am, please ensure everyone wears their body armor. It could save their lives."

"Okay, listen up. Today is going to be very difficult because of what we are going to attempt and also because of the area they are in. Sergeant Mesa will coordinate the assault. Sergeant Mesa, the floor is yours."

"I know every one of you knows your job, and I am not here to tell you how to do it. But I do know Jackson, and I know how he thinks. You can expect on the initial assault to run into heavy gunfire from every direction, so use all cover and concealment. People, please remember this is for real, and don't try to be John Wayne. Just do what you have been trained to do. After the initial assault, you can expect all sorts of traps. I do know José knows how to use explosives. He was trained as a mercenary. You can expect Claymore mines and deadfalls. Just don't trust anything to be what it appears to be. Are there any questions? Okay, Lieutenant, thanks."

"There you have it. Let's get to it. I will be in the control vehicle with the state police and the local police. Please, everyone, be careful and watch out for each other."

"Savalas, have you been on one of these before?"

"No, I haven't, and I must admit, I am scared to death."

"I am always a little afraid every time I put on my gun and uniform. I know I am just human and my time could be up at any minute. I just pray to God to spare me for another day."

"Well, Dan, we are here. It's time to get serious."

"Sergeant Mesa, Lieutenant Osborne here, move your people and stay in radio contact. We are going to assault in military fashion. I know you carry some grenades with you, so use them if you have to, over."

"Lieutenant, be careful and remember Jackson believes in setting booby traps."

"Everyone, let's move out and be careful and as quiet as a mouse."

"José, this is Martha. The police are moving in. When do we start firing?"

"Martha, let them get closer and then start firing. Make every shot count!"

"José, this is Jaime. Man, these guys are loaded for bear, and some of them have grenades. What do you want us to do?"

"Jaime, don't lose your head and don't panic."

"Don't lose my head? It's not my head I am afraid of losing, it is my life I am afraid of losing!"

"Okay, Jaime, just hold on!"

"Okay, pour it on!"

"Lieutenant, it appears Jackson has decided to die with his boots on. The only problem is, there are women up there—well, at least one. His cousin Martha is there because she hate my guts and will do anything to get even with me"

"Sergeant, if she is there, then she is part of the problem and we have to treat her the same as anyone else. We don't want to shoot anyone if it can be prevented, yet we don't want to get shot either. Do what you have to do."

"José, Martha, Jaime, Miguel, and Sammie, , this is Dan Mesa of the Arizona Rangers. Put down your guns and surrender or we will commence firing. You have until the count of five to surrender."

"Dan, you are wasting your time, because we are not surrendering and you have chosen a bad day to die."

"Martha, any day is a bad day to die. I would much rather see you live than die. As I said before, put down your guns and surrender. Your time is up. We are opening fire."

"Open fire!"

It is amazing how ignorant people are. They would rather die over something as ridiculous as family honor. I am in no rush to die. It will come soon enough. I really hate killing and today is a bad day to die.

"José, I am hit! José!"

"Jaime, are you hit bad?"

"*Si*, I am hit very bad and I need a doctor. I am bleeding all over the place. José, get me out of here, please!"

"Dan!"

"Hold your fire."

"Okay, José, what do you want?"

"Dan, Jaime is hit bad. Is it okay if Sammie brings him down?"

"José, just this once. If anyone else is hit, we will not cease firing the next time. All of you! This is a good time to surrender your weapons."

"Bring him down, Sammie, but you'd better leave your weapon where it is!"

"Ranger, this is Sammie thanks for taking care of Jaime. I do surrender."

"Savalas, handcuff him and take him to the lieutenant."

"José, Sammie has surrendered. It's your play—what are you going to do?"

"Go to hell, Ranger!"

"José, are you nuts?"

"Look, all of you. You decided to join me here. So either you stay through the end or leave now, because if you desert me when this starts again, I will shoot you myself. Who wants to leave?"

"Cousin, I love you but this is too much. I am leaving but I am not giving up. I am going to escape over those hills behind us and go to Mexico. Good luck to all of you."

We have given them enough time. I have to end this now. "Open fire!"

"Lieutenant, we gave them a chance to surrender, but they refused."

"Sergeant, the governor has instructed us to capture Jackson at all cost. Do you know what that means?"

"Yes, ma'am, I do. It means we give no quarter."

I wish José would just give up. I don't want to kill him. There has been enough killing.

"Miguel, are you hit?"

"José, this is Dan. He is dead and Martha has been hit also. Call this thing off!"

"Savalas, send in the tear gas. Everyone put on your gas masks."

"DAN MESA! You bastard, I am sending out everyone and this time it is between you and me. What do you say?"

"Okay, José, but I will not go easy on you. How do you want it?"

"High noon, like in the movies."

Lieutenant Osborne looks at a Mesa and Says; "Sergeant, are you out of you mind? You can't do it. He could kill you."

"I know. But this has to end now!"

"Jackson, send down Martha, Carlos, and Miguel right now!"

"Miguel is dead, but Martha and Carlos are coming down."

"Hold your fire until they get down."

"Martha, Carlos, you picked the wrong side this time, and you will pay for it."

"Dan Mesa, I hope you rot in hell, you no good son of a bitch."

"Martha, I didn't start this. He did but I will end it."

Corporal Dixon yells; "Sergeant, duck! Jackson flanked us. Oh my goodness. Dan are you okay?"

Dixon radios Lieutenant Osborne saying; "Lieutenant, Sergeant Mesa has been hit. Jackson shot him as he sent down his relatives."

Lieutenant Osborne is furious and says; "Dixon, throw in the grenades and level that place."

Dixon thinking to himself says; "They say hell is like this. Look at the fire. There isn't anything glorious about death and injuries. It would be great if mankind could find another way of solving his problems rather than killing."

"Lieutenant, this is Corporal Dixon. Jackson has escaped again. We need to get Sergeant Mesa to a doctor. He has been hit, and I believe it is serious."

I've been hit and they are taking me to the hospital. Jackson is on the run and he knows his chances of survival decrease every day. He has shot me and murdered four people. He is also responsible for his cousin Miguel's death.

As the ambulance arrives at the hospital the EMT says; "Doctor, we have a gunshot wound involving a Ranger. He was shot in the side and it looks bad."

"Get him to the emergency room and get Nurse Jane Evans."

"I am Lieutenant Osborne of the Yuma Company of Rangers. Please let me know how he is doing as soon as possible. I have to call his captain and the colonel."

"Lieutenant, as soon as we have a look at him, I will have someone give an update."

"Thank you, doctor."

"Captain Johnson, Lieutenant Osborne here. I have bad news to tell you. Sergeant Mesa has been shot."

"How bad is it and where is he?"

"Captain, he has a side wound and is in the hospital here. I am waiting on a report from the doctor."

"Lieutenant, as soon as you learn anything, let me know. How did this happen?"

"Sir, we were assaulting Jackson's location and Jackson asked Dan if he could send down his two cousins. Dan agreed to hold fire until they were down. In the meantime, while we were waiting, he flanked us and shot Sergeant Mesa. Captain, it wasn't an accident. Jackson intentionally shot Sergeant Mesa. I believe he wanted to murder Sergeant Mesa because Mesa is the one person who can capture him. The sergeant knows his habits better than anyone."

"Lieutenant, I will call the colonel and ask for a nationwide all-points bulletin on Jackson. The only place he is going is to hell. I will be in touch in a few minutes."

"Colonel Grant, Captain Johnson from Nogales is on the line. He seems quite upset."

"Okay, Helena, put him through.

"Sam, what is the problem?"

"Sir, Sergeant Mesa was shot over in Yuma trying to capture Jackson. He is in the emergency room at the Yuma hospital."

"Captain, what in the name of Hanna happened and how serious is he?"

"Colonel, his condition is serious, according to Lieutenant Osborne of the Yuma Company. Apparently they had cornered Jackson and his family just northwest of Yuma. Jackson asked Dan to allow his cousins to surrender and Dan agreed. While they were waiting, Jackson flanked them and shot Sergeant Mesa. The lieutenant believes Jackson intentionally shot Mesa in an attempt to kill him."

"Captain, I am issuing an all-points bulletin for Jackson dead or alive with a hundred thousand dollar reward. I want that man off the streets. I am issuing a shoot-to-kill order."

"Colonel, are you sure you want to do that?"

"Sam, I have had it with Jackson. I will take the heat for whatever happens."

"Okay, sir, and I will keep you informed about Dan's condition."

"Lieutenant, Captain Johnson here. Colonel Grant has issued an all-points bulletin for Jackson. He offered a reward of one hundred thousand dollars dead or alive. He is really pissed off."

"Sir, is that a good idea, making it dead or alive?"

"Lieutenant Osborne, he is the commander and accepts full responsibility for whatever happens. Anything new on Sergeant Mesa?"

"No, nothing yet. I will call you just as soon as I am told anything."

"My name is Doctor Mendes. Now that I've examined Ranger Mesa, I've found his condition not to be as serious as initially thought. He has an eighty percent chance of recovery and should be up and about in a week. He is a remarkable man. Now all of you get some rest and sleep."

"Corporal Savalas, Sergeant Mesa is resting easily and has an eighty percent chance of recovery. The wound isn't as serious as we thought. Is there anyone we need to notify about what happened?"

"Lieutenant, his mother is elderly and lives in Louisiana, but he also has a brother who is a policeman in Louisiana. I will notify him and he can tell their mother."

Dan Mesa, what have you done now? Here you are, lying here with a hole in your side, wondering what is next. I wonder what would have happened if I had chosen a different profession. I probably should have taken that job in Turkey and returned to teaching college. I swear to this. Jackson is one dead man, and I will show no mercy to him or anyone who shelters him.

Lieutenant Osborne enters. "Dan Mesa, you really scared the daylights out of me. I am so relieved that you are okay. I called

Captain Johnson and he called Colonel Grant. The short of it is, there is a fifty-thousand-dollar reward for Jackson dead or alive and an all-points bulletin has been issued. I know you are in pain, so I won't stay long. Here is a hug and a kiss to let you know I care about you more than you know."

"Alana, thanks for caring and yes, I do know how you feel. If I were sane, I would fall madly in love with you. So just hang in there. I am in a lot of pain, but it is mental pain and anguish. I plan to kill Jackson as soon as I can get out of this bed. I swear to you and the Rangers he will be dead before this month is out. I am not too sure what I will do afterward. I may leave the Rangers."

"Dan, don't do anything rash. Think about what you are saying. I will be back tomorrow."

"Captain Johnson, Dan is awake and it appears he will be okay. He is exhausted, but what I am worried about is his mental state. Captain, he has changed, and what I saw in his eyes really worries me. He has the look of a wild animal—like a timber wolf. He has vowed to kill Jackson before the month is out. He also mentioned leaving the Rangers afterward."

"Lieutenant, you seem to care more than a little about Dan Mesa. I will tell you, it is not to your advantage to get a case on him. He is not ready for an involvement yet. I think after this Jackson thing is over, he will be. Now, about leaving the Rangers. I don't think you will have to worry about that. Dan Mesa dearly loves this organization, and he will not leave it, at least not right now anyway. If he does leave, it will be because he retires, not because of this Jackson situation."

"Captain, Savalas mentioned a lady named Sonia Perdenales and what happened in Tucson. Will you please give her a call and tell her what happened here?"

"Will do, Lieutenant. Keep me informed and I will call the colonel."

"Sonia, Captain Johnson here. I am calling to tell you that Dan was shot, but he is okay. Now don't panic, and no, he isn't going to die. He is conscious and talking."

"Captain Johnson, I am guilty of being extremely stupid. I guess you know what happened in Tucson and how I reacted. I must apologize to him for my behavior. I am beginning to believe he is something special to me. I have been extremely stupid."

"Sonia, he understood, and believe me, he does care about you although he may be slow in revealing it. He will recover but be aware of something. Dan may change. He may develop a hatred of Jackson. He has already said he plans to kill Jackson before the month is out. He is changing already, and he will be more dangerous than he is now."

"Thanks for calling, Captain Johnson. I will try to call him."

Sonia hangs up and thinks for a moment. "What do I say to him after the way I acted? I am not a child but sometimes I react like one. He will probably hate me also."

"Hello Savalas this is Dan, how are you? How is the manhunt going?"

"Dan, I'm okay, but I am worried about you, as everyone is. Are you in pain?"

"No, I am not in pain. Again, how is the manhunt going?"

"We have had reports that José has crossed over into Mexico. If he has, we have a problem."

"No, Mike, he hasn't left the United States yet. Jackson does not like Mexico, so he is still here somewhere and I will find him sooner or later. When I do, I will end his criminal career once and for all."

"Dan, as a friend I am asking you to go slowly, because your injury is worse than you think. You are not ten feet tall and bulletproof!"

"Mike, I know that, and believe me, I am not going to do anything stupid. I plan to live a long time. I was not careless, and what happened could not have been avoided. It is the chance you take when you put on this badge. Jackson was my friend and what I did—allowing his family to surrender—was the right thing to do. He played the coward's hand and shot me and that is unforgivable. I will kill him unless God changes my mind."

" Nurse Evans walks in and says; "Ranger, get out and let my patient rest—and you, go to sleep! I don't want you lying around here goofing off when you could be doing your job."

"Thanks, ma'am, for your help. I will be out of here by the end of the week. I'm not seriously injured, and I do heal quickly."

"Ranger, you are extremely lucky that that bullet didn't hit any vital organs. Normally a wound of the type you have means death. God was on your side. You must live right."

Meanwhile in another location unknown to the Ranger a scene is played out.

"José, I am your momma and I told you what would happen if you carried through with your plan. You tried twice to kill your best friend, and now you've shot the man who loved you like a brother. What will it take to satisfy you? You know your life won't be worth a wooden nickel. Daniel Mesa will kill you now. I know this man and how he thinks, and right about now he is planning your execution."

"Momma, I don't know what to do now. Everything is so jumbled up. It wasn't supposed to be like this."

"My son, all of this is your doing. You didn't need money so desperately that you had to steal it. One bad act often leads to another."

"Dad, what would you do if you were me?"

"José, you need to go someplace where he can't find you. Someplace far away and where no one will see you or be able to report you. The only place I know of is the Four Corners area. Head to that location and hide out, and then slip across the border if you want to live."

"Dan will hunt me all the way to Colorado. He is worse than a hound dog on a scent. He will kill me unless I kill him first. I don't plan to die. I'll admit I should have handled things differently, but it is too late now. You know, if anyone had told me five years ago that I would shoot the man who was my best friend, I would have told them where to go. Now I am just another lost soul."

"Son, you created this situation, and now you have to deal with it. It is time for you to get moving. I will see you when I see you."

If I were Jackson, where would I hide out? He will not stay in Yuma, and he will not go back to Tucson, so where? It will have to be in a location that is almost inaccessible by car or foot. If it were me, I'd go into the mountains and stay there. He could live for months there and not be seen. The Four Corners area is the most isolated area. That's where Jackson will head, and that's where I am going.

"Ranger, a Mrs. Osborne is calling for you. Do you want to speak to her?"

The nurse hands me the phone and my hands are shaking. Maybe I am not ready just yet.

"Mrs. Osborne, how you doing?"

She is really concerned and says, "Ranger, I don't have so many friends that I can afford to lose one. You brought back memories of my husband, and I haven't slept since I was told about your incident. I know Alana is almost cracking up over this. She set store by you, sir. We must talk when you are better. Dan, I think you are tops, but you lead a dangerous life. Do you understand why I am concerned?"

I have that sinking feeling in my stomach again. "Yes, ma'am, I understand why you are concerned. I admit Alana deserves better, and so do you. I will exit gracefully, and I won't take things any farther."

"Dan, this is hard for me because I care about you in the same way. She told me what you said and that makes me care about you even more, but neither one of us can go through that again." She hangs up.

I seem to be making a real mess of things lately. I can't seem to get things right. It is time for me to move on anyway. I've been around too long.

"Ranger Mesa, there is a Captain Johnson on the line for you. Do you feel up to talking to him?"

"Yes, ma'am, I will take it."

"Hello, Captain, I am feeling much better. I should be out of here in a couple of days."

"Sergeant Mesa, I sent you to Yuma to hurt Jackson, not for Jackson to hurt you. I can't afford to lose a good man. Do I need to take you off this case? Has it gotten too personal?" "Captain, this is just another job involving a lawbreaker, and I will capture him one way or another," I say. "What happened could not have been prevented unless I had decided to disregard the lives of his relatives, whose only crime was trying to help him. I didn't want them. I only want him. I'll let the local police deal with them.""Dan, of course you were right to do what you did; I am not second-guessing you on that. What I am concerned about is how this will affect you when it is all over. I know you better than you think I do, and I know you are bound and determine to get José. Three times he has tried to kill you, and I know you and how you feel about betrayal. Can you continue as a Ranger when this is over?"

"Sir, I will admit I don't handle betrayal well, especially from someone who was as close to me as a brother. What really galls me is that he tried to murder me when I was only trying to help his family after he asked me to. That I will never forgive, come hell or high water."

The captain calmly says to me, "Dan, don't upset yourself. Just get better and get on with what you have to do. Sonia was told about you. She is very concerned, and she is sorry about how she reacted. I told her you understood why she acted as she did. You do understand, don't you?"

I am somewhat dumbfounded, in that I thought it was over. I answer, "Yes, I do understand, but I am surprised she called. I thought she was through with me."

"Ranger, for a smart man you are dumb when it comes to the fairer sex. That lady is crazy about you even if she doesn't know it yet."

I find myself smiling. "Thank you, sir," I say. What will I do now? I must get well and get out of here and get on with what I started out doing.

Lieutenant Osborne is having a difficult time dealing with the situation at hand and is having a long talk with her mother.

"Mom, I am responsible for Dan's injuries. I should have had the guys more alert and responding to the situation. I failed and he was shot. He could have been killed!"

Her mom listens and finally answers, "Lieutenant Osborne, my daughter, you did what you thought was right. You did everything right and you saved lives. What is important is that you acted correctly. Daniel Mesa is an extraordinary guy, and I know how you feel about him. He reminds me of your father, which is why I can't get involved with him and you can't either. I know you have feelings for him also. I spoke with him today and told him how I felt and that I thought the two of you shouldn't see each other again."

"I know you are right, Mom, but it doesn't make me feel any better. He is one of the really good guys. They are hard to find. What do we do about him now?"

"Sweetheart, we'll keep him in our hearts and pray that he remains safe from danger. He is one of a kind like your dad was. Dan Mesa is the only man I've looked at with interest since your father's death. I don't think there will ever be another."

Alana says, "Mom, you shouldn't let him get away. He needs someone, and you need a life of your own. You are still young. I know he has been through a lot and is hurting badly, and so are you.

I love you, Mom, and I am here for you."

"I know, sweetheart, and I am here for you also."

Dan Mesa is slowly recovering from his wound. He has been released from the hospital and is recovering at his home. He has more friends than he realizes. Mesa realizes it is time to call home and reaches for the phone but it rings as he is reaching.

"Hello, David, it is good to hear from you. Yes, I am recovering fast. The hospital allowed me to come home today. How is Mom handling all of this?"

"Well, Dan, you know how she is. She is still as strong and bullheaded as ever. I do believe this incident scared her a bit, and I know it scared me. You have to promise me to be a bit more careful in the future. I can't afford to lose a brother."

"Thanks, Dave. I thought I was being careful. José used to be a good friend, but somewhere along the way he changed into a vicious killer. He intentionally tried to kill me, and that I don't forgive."

"Dan, I know you and I know how mean you can get. Take it easy and don't do anything you'll regret. Stay within the law—both God's law and man's law. I don't want you doing anything to get yourself sent to prison."

"Dave, I promise I will stay within the law, but I will send him to hell unless he turns himself in. The colonel issued a shoot-to-kill order for Jackson. I won't shoot unless he refuses to surrender."

"Okay, Dan. Just be careful and don't allow your anger to overrule common sense. Take care and I will talk to you."

"Ranger headquarters, Sergeant Mendosa speaking."

"Mendosa, Dan Mesa here. Is the captain in his office?

"Hold on, Dan, I'll check and see."

"Captain Johnson, Sergeant Mesa is on the line for you."

"Put him through."

"Sergeant, how are you and what can I do for you?"

"Sir, just wanted to let you know I have been discharged from the hospital and I am at my house here in Nogales."

"It is good you are okay and that you have been discharged. Have you called Sonia? I know she'd like to talk to you."

"Well, I've given thought to calling her, but I haven't gotten the nerve to do so yet. I guess now is as good a time as any. Captain, I will be in to talk to you soon. Thanks."

There are times in this life of mine when I find it hard to understand the human being, myself included. Why do we do the things we do? I know we are not quite what God wants us to be, but then I guess that is why we are just humans.

"Hello, may I speak with Sonia Perdenales? This is Dan Mesa."

"Sonia, he is on the phone and wants to talk to you!"

"Who is on the phone, Mesha?"

"It's that Ranger fella, Dan Mesa!"

"Oh, okay, I'll take it!"

"Hello, Dan, how are you? Are you feeling okay? I mean, have you been released from the hospital?"

"Yes, I have been released and I am okay and at home here in Nogales. I am calling to find out if you are okay and to apologize for the situation I got you involved in. What happened was not intended, and I just reacted as I have been conditioned to do. It was the second time someone had tried to shoot me."

"There isn't any need to apologize, Dan. I know it wasn't your fault. It was something that happened because of José's behavior. I just acted like a child, and for that I apologize. I have been worried about you since the shooting. I was too ashamed and too afraid to call you. I thought maybe you would not want to see me again because of the way I acted."

"Sonia, one of the reasons I am calling you is to ask you to have dinner with me on Friday night."

"Oh, well, yes, I would love to have dinner with you. I promise not to get crazy this time."

"My dear lady, you weren't crazy before. Things just have a way of happening around me. I will see you on Friday then. Bye."

Mesha says, "Sonia, isn't he that gunslinging Ranger that everyone talks about? I hear he has killed five or six people. What is he all about?"

"Mesha, he is a very nice person and I like him a lot. More than I thought possible. He has killed in the line of duty, but he has never murdered anyone and he is not a gunslinger. It is as if trouble just follows him around. He was shot in Yuma a few weeks ago by José Gutierrez-Jackson, you know, the guy who shot Marshal Huitt over in Patagonia. Now Dan will kill Jackson, a man who was once his best friend. He is hurting a lot and there isn't anything I can do to help him."

"Sonia, he and the Rangers raided Los Negritos and he shot a guy there. They say he drew that gun so fast you couldn't blink fast enough. He then commenced to fight like a banshee—and you like him? Rumor has it he spent time in Vietnam and the Persian Gulf War. Does he like killing or something? I would be afraid of him!"

Sonia knows about the rumors floating around about Mesa but prefers to keep an open mind. "Mesha he has a most difficult job, one that entails being among some of society's most deviant personalities and

73

the worst people society can produce. I was married to a policeman before and he was killed doing the same things Dan does every day. I chose to marry my husband knowing what his job was. I like Dan and yes, I do worry, but I believe he is worth the worry. He was in Vietnam and in the Persian Gulf. I do know he hates to kill, but I also know he is darned good at it and that is how he has survived as long as he has. He is probably fifty-one years old and looks like he is about thirty-five. He has been through a lot and that is why he has such sad eyes."

"Girl, you have a crush on him, don't you?"

"Mesha, that is the problem. I am not sure how he feels about me. I don't want to rush into anything, and I know he is hesitant because of his past experiences. I do know I'd miss him if he went away and didn't come back. I went through hell after I found out he had been shot. When I see his face, I will know more about his feelings about me and life in general."

"If he is coming by to pick you up for dinner on Friday, then maybe I will see him and can give you my seal of approval."

Sonia looks at Mesha with a smile and says, "Oh really? You will be the only friend that has seen him. It will be great to have your opinion of him! I do hope you like him."

Dan Mesa is a man at a crossroads in his life and doesn't quite know what to do about it. He has met a lady he likes but is afraid to say so. He may have to kill an old friend who has become a fugitive from justice accused of at least four and one attempted murder of a police officer. Dan has to decide if he is willing to risk his life to bring José in alive or kill him with the least possible risk. No one ever said life is fair. You pay your dime and you take your chances.

I think I will go and feed the horses. I haven't ridden them in a long time. My gosh, I need to call the vet and check on Red and see how his wounds are mending. I still owe José for shooting Red. "Hello, Brandy, old girl. How are we today? I must apologize for not riding you and Charley, but I have been somewhat busy these last few days. I promise I will do better after this affair is over."

Ah, the phone is ringing. "Hello? Oh, hi, Lieutenant Osborne, how are you and your mom?"

"Okay. Dan, get off the formalities. This isn't a formal call. I am calling on a personal note. How are you feeling? Are you healing both physically and psychologically?"

"Alana, I am okay. I am not deranged or anything remotely similar. I am okay and ready to return to duty. How is your mom and how are you?"

"Mom is well and so am I. We both miss you. It seems as if we have known you for a long time. It was just nice having you here in Yuma. I guess both Mom and I are a little in love with you. I just want you to know that you have two friends who care deeply about you. We are here if you ever need us."

"Alana, if there was only one of you, then I would be in love with you, but there are two of you and I love you both deeply. I discovered that while in the hospital. I could never come between you and your mom. I care too much about both of you. She is absolutely gorgeous and so are you. I will be up to see you before too long."

"Dan, we love you also. Take care."

Those two women are a delight and I will always have deep feelings for them. I sometimes wish things were different or I was different. No, I don't, not really. I am happy with myself without any serious changes. I feel fortunate that two women have accepted me as I am.It is Friday morning. What do I do with myself? I should call Savalas and check to see what is new with José.

Ranger Savalas has been trying to keep a trace on Gutierrez-Jackson but has run into a dead end. No one has anything to say. All information seems to have just dried up. At Ranger headquarters Captain Johnson is getting a little upset.

"Rangers, there are at least two hundred of us scattered throughout twenty-six companies around this state and thousands of other law enforcement officers, and no one can find hide or hair of Jackson? I find that to be utterly unacceptable! Find a bloody lead! Now!"

Sergeant Mendoza, the desk sergeant, has been on the phone all morning running down leads. Finally, he is notified by the New Mexico State Police that a vehicle of José's description has been seen in Albuquerque. Mendoza knocks on the captain's door.

"Come in, Mendoza, what do you have?"

"Sir, the New Mexico police notified me that José's vehicle has been seen in Albuquerque, but they can't be sure that the driver was José, so they are investigating."

"Okay, Mendoza, get back with them, find out if it is José they are following, and let me know immediately."

Meanwhile, in Albuquerque in a hotel on Wyoming Street, José and his companion Frank Stillwell are discussing their future. "Frank, I have to get completely out of this part of the country. Dan Mesa will never give up on me as long as he lives. One day he will find me and I will be dead. I tried having him killed and I tried to kill him twice myself. Each time he has survived. He was the best friend I ever had or could hope to have. Now he is my worst enemy, and I wish he were still my best friend. However, I will kill him if I get the chance."

"José, you are a piece of work. This Ranger and you were best friends and you try knocking him off three times? Man, are you crazy or something? I would hate for either of you to be after me. So where do you want to go next?"

"I have been thinking about going to Colorado and buying a small place there and raising sheep and a few cows. I know about forestry management and could probably get a job with the Forest Service. I'd have to change my name and that could be a problem."

Stillwell says, "José, that's a good idea. I know about ranching and could get a job on a ranch. If we maintain a low profile, we can blend in and just get on with our lives. Maybe the law will forget about us."

The clock of events is moving slowly but steadily, and Jackson and Stillwell are sitting on a powder keg. In Ranger headquarters in Yuma, Major McMasters has been brought up to date on the situation. The major asks, "What are we doing right now to find Jackson and apprehend him?"

Lieutenant Osborne enters the office at that point and explains, "Sir, I was just notified by Captain Johnson of Santa Cruz Company that Jackson and his friend Frank Stillwell were spotted in Albuquerque by the police, who are actively looking for him. There is an all-points bulletin out on Jackson throughout the Southwest. I have a feeling Jackson will leave this area and head someplace north to hide out or go to Mexico. I believe we should have the Colorado State Police on the lookout for Jackson and also the Border Patrol."

"Osborne, you could be right, because nothing seems to be working when it comes to Jackson. That man has got to be the luckiest person in the world or he has an angel on his side. He should have been caught long ago, and we keep missing him even though we are doing everything right. Today is Friday, and as of this moment all Rangers are on twelve-hour shifts until further notice."

In Nogales Dan Mesa is busy doing what he likes best, tending to his horses. He'd like to ride but because of the injury he received, he knows better than to ride. He talks to the horses in a soft, coaxing voice. "Okay, old girl, it has been a few days since we have gone riding but soon. Soon I will be back to one hundred percent and we will tear those hills up. We will take a canter along that ridge over there and ride into hills and camp out for a while. Nell, old girl, there are many miles of desert you and I could take and get lost. Maybe we will take Old Ben along also. He can be the packhorse for that trip. Ben, you get well and we'll go mountain fishing."

The phone rings and Dan answers. "Hello."

"Hello, Dan, this is Sonia. I am calling to find out if you're well and feeling okay. I am concerned about you, and I think you need to spend the night at my place."

"Well, ah, ah, I, I . . . Well, okay."

"Dan Mesa, I do believe I embarrassed you. Do you think I am shameless?"

After regaining his composure, Dan Mesa says, "No, Sonia, I don't think you are shameless, not by a long shot. It is just that I've not been close to anyone in so long that I'd forgotten how nice it feels for someone to ask me to stay the night."

"Dan, I am not being pushy or forward. I like you a lot and I will not lose you without a fight. I have not invited anyone to stay the night since my husband's death. I guess it is time for a change for both of us. I am not asking you to move in, only to stay the night with a friend. I know how you value your independence. So, what do you think of my proposal?"

With a smile, which is seldom seen on Ranger Mesa's face, he answers, "I accept and I thank you for caring about me. It has been a while since anyone cared that much about me. I am told I am a difficult person to care for. I am in the barn caring for my horses.

Ben is the one that was shot a few days ago. He is up and about now but not ready for working yet. We have been together for ten years. I raised him from a colt."

"Daniel Mesa, I am trying to proposition you and all you can talk about is your horse? Am I not important to you?"

What do I say to her? She is very important, and I can't lose her. "Sonia, I am trying to say that I would love to spend nights and days with you. I am making a mess of things, I know, but I do want you to know how much I care about you. I guess I am totally smitten with you."

Sonia, with a smile in her voice, says, "Dan, I thought you loved me and you were or are too shy to say it."

"Yes, you are somewhat correct. I won't say I love you just yet, but you are definitely in the ballpark."

Inside of Dan Mesa's psyche is a confusion of feelings and emotion. He has been at this point in life before and knows he can't trust anything that is happening. In the past, this moment has proven to be as quicksilver, not lasting.

"Dan, why are you so afraid of getting close to anyone?"

"Sonia, I think the world of you and you know that, but I just can't discuss that right now. I promise you I will tell you everything and we will discuss it until you are satisfied, but not right now. Please?"

"All right, Dan, but I will hold you to it."

"What time should I show up at your house this evening?"

"Ranger, you are welcome at my campfire anytime you show up."

At the Ranger station in Nogales, Captain Johnson is on the phone with Colonel Grant. "Sam, I have heard that Jackson is in Albuquerque. Do we have any confirmation of that?"

"Yes, sir, the New Mexico State Police said they spotted Jackson's truck and they are watching him. Sir, Dan is recovering fast and I am going to send him and Savalas to Albuquerque to work with the state police in apprehending Jackson. However, I don't believe he is still in Albuquerque. I believe he is too smart for that. If I took a guess, I'd say he is in the mountains somewhere in the Four Corners. He knows he needs to be in an area where he is not easily accessed."

The colonel replies, "Sam, are you sure Mesa is ready, both physically and mentally, to go back to work?"

"Yes, I do, because I know the sergeant better than anyone. He is ready, and nothing short of death could stop him from going after Jackson. Yes, sir, he is definitely ready to go back into action."

"Okay, Sam, when do you plan to send him to Albuquerque?"

"Today is Friday, so I want him in place by Tuesday."

In Yuma, Lieutenant Alana Osborne is agonizing over her life, trying to figure out what to do. She believes she is in love with Dan Mesa but knows there are some serious obstacles to their happiness.

In Amado, Sonia Perdenales is as happy as a meadowlark. She is waiting for the arrival of Dan Mesa from Nogales. Her friend Mesha is present also.

"Sonia, is he really coming here?"

"Yes, Mesha, he is coming and I can barely wait to see him again!"

"Well, unless I miss my guess, he is arriving right now. Does he drive a beige Toyota truck?"

"Yes, he does, and you are right, he has arrived. What do you think of him?"

"Sonia, he is handsome although somewhat short. I like his looks. He looks as if he just stepped out of the pages of western history. He has the gun, the walk, and that air of self-control. I can see how he could be interesting. How is he in bed?"

"Mesha, I can't believe you asked that! We have been out together only once, and that turned out bad. Although I must admit I have wondered about that. Anyway, not a word from you about that, okay?"

Sonia and Mesha proceed to the door to greet the famous Dan Mesa.

"Hello, Ranger, and welcome to my humble abode. This is my friend and little sister, Mesha."

"Hello, Mesha, I am Dan Mesa."

Mesha smiles a wicked smile and says, "Yes, you are most definitely Dan Mesa, that super guy I have heard so much about."

"Dan, Mesha is a pain. Don't pay any attention to her. She exaggerates things.

"Dan, how about us going to the Cow Palace tonight, to eat and just hang out there? It is where we met, and I would like to return there with you."

"I'd like that also and the food is good. I've had as much of my cooking as I can stand, and a good steak would really do wonders for me. Mesha, I hope you will be joining us. Any friend of Sonia is welcome at my campfire anytime."

"Ranger, you have yourself a date with two beautiful women. You are the most fortunate man alive. You do know Sonia talks about you only all the time. According to her, you are a cross between Wyatt Earp and Chuck Norris. Anyway, anyone who makes this lady smile and anyone who can entice her to go out must be okay. So, I am really happy to make your acquaintance."

"Does that mean I pass the test?" Mesa asks with a smile.

"Dan, you passed the Mesha Santamaria test of sincerity."

Mesha looks at Mesa and says, "Ranger, are you aware that you have a reputation bigger than life? They say you are, let us say, the last of a breed. They say you are incorruptible and that you can't be bought. It is also said that you are the best friend a person can have. How much of it is true? My dad and brother say you are exactly what this part of the country needs. As long as you are good to Sonia and treat her right, you are okay with me."

Dan Mesa is usually the one who puts others on the spot, but suddenly he finds himself on the defensive or in the hot seat, and it is very uncomfortable. He gives that Mesa smile and says, "I am suddenly without words to express how I feel. I can assure you, though, that I care a lot about Sonia, and I guess I have since we first met."

Sonia is feeling the heat also. Her face is glowing after Dan makes his remarks.

"Ranger Mesa, I didn't know you felt that way, but I am most pleased," she says with a smile.

"Ladies, I guess we should head out for dinner—my treat. I have been eating my own cooking and I could use a break. The Cow Palace is one of my favorite places, along with Pete's Kitchen. I like the history surrounding both places."

Mesha's curiosity gets the better of her and she asks, "Dan, how did a man like you ever wind up here in Arizona as a Ranger? You are different from most men I know."

"Mesha, I assume you are asking how a person of color wound up here and working as an Arizona Ranger. I was born in New Orleans to Creole parents. Creoles are people of African, French, Spanish, and Native American background. My grandfather was born a slave in New Orleans in 1850 and actually served in the Civil War as a boy. He married my grandmother and my father was born in 1897. Around 1900 my grandparents moved to Oklahoma. My father later settled in north Louisiana, where I was born. I grew up on stories of the Texas Rangers and the Twenty-Six Men, the original Arizona Rangers, and I wanted to become one. After serving my twenty in the air force, I retired here and Captain Johnson hired me. Before joining the air force I worked the rodeo circuit throughout South Texas and New Mexico and parts of Arizona, and I fell in love with the Arizona desert and the sunset. The rest is history."

"Yes, but black men don't usually act and dress as you do. Why are you what you are?"

"Well, ladies, we are here at last and off to a great dinner."

"Sergeant Mesa, you were saved by the bell."

"Good evening, Sonia, and Ranger Mesa, I believe?"

"Oh, Trudy, this is Sergeant Daniel Mesa of the Arizona Rangers, and you know Mesha. Dan, this is Trudy, my friend and the night manager of the Palace."

"My pleasure, ma'am."

Trudy seats them and takes their drink order. Dan orders wine for the ladies and himself. Trudy returns with the drinks and orders are taken. The ladies order shrimp, chicken, and vegetables, and Mesa orders trout amandine.

"Dan, the last time you were here was the one moment in my life when I felt totally without words to express myself so I just passed you that note, remember?"

"Yes, I do remember, and I remember how surprised I was. I couldn't believe that a lady like you wanted to talk to a guy like me. I have a lot of confidence in myself when it comes to my job or anything of that nature. However, when it comes to affairs of the heart, I am at a loss. I find that I have no confidence at all. I am always afraid the lady will not feel the way I feel, so I keep my distance. I am very happy you decided to speak to me. I am a most fortunate man."

Mesha is amazed at the two of them and says, "You two are absolutely meant for each other. Dan, Sonia hasn't spoken to a man with any interest in over two years. You are the first man in whom she has shown interest. You must be someone special, and from what I see, you need her as much as she needs you. I know something of your reputation as a lawman, and it paints a picture of a hard-nosed person with no give in him. Now that I see you, you are completely different. How is this possible?"

Dan suddenly becomes aware he is vulnerable and chooses his words carefully. "Mesha, I sometimes exclude others from my life and refuse to get involved with anyone for fear of getting hurt. I have been through the ringer a few times and I can't go through it again. In the past I just kept everyone at a distance. I can't tell you I am cured of that ailment, not even now. I am taking it one day at a time."

The food arrives and a pleasant meal follows with delightful conversation. The conversation steers itself to José Gutierrez-Jackson when Mesha asks, "Ranger, how is the hunt for Jackson going?"

A look of sadness appears on the Ranger's face. Sonia and Mesha see the change and Sonia comments. "Dan, why the sad face?"

"I guess I feel a sense of sadness when I think of Jackson. We were such good friends in a different place and at a different time. It is always a sad day when a good person becomes a bad person."

"Ranger, you and Jackson were friends and he tried to kill you?"

"Yes, we were and yes, he tried to kill me. I will kill him the first chance I get. I won't be merciful either!"

"Dan, let's talk about something different. It brings back bad memories."

"Let's order dessert and coffee. Coffee has become a mainstay with me. During my college years, I was often broke, but I could buy a cup of coffee and three doughnuts for twenty-five cents. I developed a liking for coffee. It is my one serious weakness."

"Ranger, are you ever afraid of death or that you could be permanently injured?" Mesha asks.

"I don't think about it much. I know nothing is promised so I try to live my life in a manner so that if I do die, I will have given God my best. I know I have had to take lives in the performance of my job, and I know it goes against my religion and its practices. I have to trust that God knows best and that he knows that I stand for justice and equality under the law and that I would never intentionally take a person's life. I will even give Jackson a chance to surrender."

Sonia looks at Mesha and then at Dan and says; "I have been around a lot of police during my life and I must admit I have grown to like most of them. They give a lot and get very little in return. They are the one thing that stands between chaos and us. Their life is one of much stress and pain. The average policeman either has marriage problems or a substance abuse problem of some kind. Those who do not have a good strong spouse who understands his job and supports them suffer the most. Most police have served in some branch of the military and understand the meaning of sacrifice. It has been like that since the frontier days and before. I guess that is why Dan is often referred to as the last of a breed. Men like him are few and far in between. I believe the world is a better place because of men and womenlike him."

Sergeant Mesa of the Arizona Rangers suddenly feels that old loneliness that creeps into his mind and soul. It is always the same—alone in a crowd. Where and when will he feel content enough to relax and enjoy life? The years are slowly building up, and there only so many days and hours left. He feels the weight of the years heavily on his shoulders, but being the type of man he is, he accepts the facts of his existence and moves on.

The meal is over and it is time to take the ladies home. As they emerge from the Cow Palace, Sergeant Mesa instinctively goes on the alert. Sonia immediately notices his reaction. His hands are poised and ready, and every muscle in his body is tense and ready to react. A truck backfires, and Mesa steps in front of the ladies and draws his weapon with lightning speed, ready to open fire. He holds his fire but is still poised and ready. His sudden action frightens Mesha terribly, and Sonia panics.

Sonia, in a fit of anger, says, "Dan, what are you doing? It was only a truck backfiring. You really need help. Your reactions aren't normal."

Mesha comments, "I haven't been this scared in my entire life. I know you live a different life, but this is too much for me."

Dan quietly and calmly says, "I will take you both home."

They arrive at Sonia's place and Dan escorts them to the door and quietly says, "I will leave now and I won't be coming back this way for a while. I thank you for a pleasant evening. I live in a world different from yours. Every day I deal with all the things you and others don't want to know about. I have to associate with the scum of the earth sometimes, and you draw the line there. Well, I can't. This is who I am. Love me or hate me, nothing changes. I hoped it would be different with us. I shan't bother you again. Good night, Sonia, and it was nice meeting you, Mesha."

He abruptly turns and walks away with the weight of the world on his shoulders, a lonely man with nowhere to go and no one to go to.

Sonia watches him with tears in her eyes. She knows she should run after him, but her pride will not allow her to go. Mesha says, "There goes a real man and a gentleman. His likes will not be seen again. Sonia, go after him. Don't let him go!"

"Mesha, I know I should go after him, but I just can't get used to the idea of what he does and how he does it. He is like a coiled spring ready to snap with the least provocation. He is the best man I have ever met and the most effective law officer I have ever seen. I love him with all my heart, and yet he frightens me. He can be so violent so quickly. Did you see how fast he stepped in front of us, drawing that bloody pistol at the same time? He handles that thing like it is a part of him. He is never without it! I know he is required to carry it, but I wish he could just relax and be happy."

With her last remarks, she breaks down crying and all Mesha can do is watch two beautiful people who should be together go in opposite directions. Her heart is heavy, and the pain of seeing them torn apart is more than she wants to witness.

Dan Mesa slowly drives back to Nogales and to his small place, where there is only solitude. How much pain can one man take? How much rejection is one body to experience?

As he enters the door, the phone rings and Captain Johnson says, "Dan, Jackson has been spotted in Durango, Colorado. I know you wanted to know about it. Are you well enough to continue your pursuit of Jackson? If you are, then get up there and check in the Colorado State Police in Durango. Your contact is Colonel Hugh Justice. Stop in at Yuma and bring them up to date. Take a flight from Yuma to Durango. Call me when you get there. Sergeant, what is bothering you?"

"Nothing, sir . . . I just can't seem to get my life in order. Sonia and I are all finished, I'm afraid. I was hoping she would be my future. Tonight I took Sonia and her friend Mesha to dinner at the Cow Palace. When we were departing, a truck backfired, which sounded like a gunshot. I reacted in a manner that frightened both of them. Sonia said I need psychiatric help, and I could see it in her eyes that she didn't want any part of this life I lead. So I left and will not be seeing her again. She is a great lady and a beautiful person and deserves better than me."

"Sergeant, I can't tell you what to do on that one, but I can say that each of you is exactly what the other needs. Under the circumstances your reaction was normal. I would have reacted the same way. Good luck in Colorado, Sergeant."

"Thank you, sir. I hope we can end this thing in the next few weeks."

Dan arrives in Yuma on Saturday, July 1. The Jackson saga has been going for six weeks. Everyone associated with it is eager to end it. He checks in with Major McMasters and Lieutenant Osborne.

Lieutenant Osborne sees Mesa as he gets out of his truck and says, "Dan, it is so good to see you again. Captain Johnson called the major and informed him you were heading in this direction. I am so happy to see you. Mom will be glad to see you also."

Looking at Alana gladdens my heart and I say, "Lieutenant, it is great to see you also. I hope your mom is well and happy. I have missed both of you."

"Dan, you have that same look you had the first time I saw you. It is one of being alone. What has happened to you since you left?"

"Alana, do you remember the lady who called and checked on me while I was in the hospital? Well, she and I are finished. It happened and I don't know how to deal with it."

"Okay, so tell me what happened."

"We were at dinner and things were great. When we were leaving, a truck backfired and it sounded like a gunshot, so I reacted by drawing my weapon and pushing her out of the line of fire. She was frightened and lashed out at me. I can't go through another breakup. It will finish me."

Alana understands and says, "Dan, you have Mom and me, and we are here for you. You know how we feel about you, and we won't turn away or leave you."

Deep in Ranger Mesa's psyche he knows he is in love with Alana, but he refuses to acknowledge it. Dan reports to Major McMasters.

"Sir, Captain Johnson sent me here to bring you up to date on Jackson and to tell you that Jackson is in Durango, Colorado. I have been ordered to proceed to Durango to become a part of the investigative team. Captain Johnson thought you'd like to send someone from your detachment also."

Major McMasters replies, "Yes, I do want to send someone, and Lieutenant Osborne is the most familiar with the case, so if you don't mind, I will send her along with you."

"It will be great to work with Lieutenant Osborne again, sir."

Major McMasters sends for the lieutenant and tells her, "Alana, you will accompany the sergeant to head up the investigation of Jackson, and to make sure both of you stay alive and well. Today is Saturday, so I want you on a plane out of here by tomorrow afternoon, okay?"

Sergeant Mesa turns to Lieutenant Osborne and asks, "Lieutenant, may I leave my truck at your place while I am away?"

"Yes, Dan, and why don't you stay at the ranch tonight? I know Mom will want to see you."

"Thanks, ma'am, I do appreciate it. I will follow you home then."

As they approach Alana's place, they see Alana's mother loading up her car. "Mom, where are you going? Look who I found hanging around Yuma!"

Mrs. Osborne hurries and gives Dan a big hug and with genuine feeling says, "It is good to have you back here again. I only regret I have to meet some friends in Phoenix for the weekend. . So, the place belongs to you guys. Alana told me she is going to Durango with you to carry on the investigation. Dan, you guys be careful. I want both of you back safely. I love you both dearly."

"Mom, I promise I will take care of him and keep him out of trouble. He can't seem to manage it on his own," Alana says with a smile.

So, Adelaide Matilda Osborne leaves the two Rangers home alone. Dan turns to Alana and asks, "What do we do now?"

Alana slowly turns and says, "Dan I am in love with you and I don't care who knows it. I missed you terribly. I know you have had a rough time of it, but I promise you I am on the level and that I will love you always. I know this is sudden and I—"

"Alana, Alana! If you will allow me to speak, I have something to say to you also. I missed you terribly. I must tell you up front that Sonia means a lot to me also, but I don't think she can adjust to my way of life. She can't deal with the violence in this job. I don't blame her at all. I just thought she'd be my future. I can't tell you I love you so suddenly. I would be less than a man to do that. When I am free of her, then I will come to you free of other entanglements. That does not mean that I don't want to be with you. I just can't say I love you right now."

"Dan Mesa, you are a hard man to understand. I know how you feel better than you do. I know you love me dearly and you have since we first met. You just haven't realized it yet. Okay, I will wait until you are ready. But just remember I am here. This kiss is to show you what is missing in your life."

She gives the Ranger a kiss that is so pleasant that Sergeant Mesa of the Arizona Rangers feels his legs going weak. He knows everything she has said is true, but he must be true to himself. After the kiss he says to her, "Alana, I, well, I just want to say that— What I really mean is—"

Alana interrupts him and says in the sweetest voice, "Dan, I know what you are trying to say. I just wanted you to know what you are missing, and I do believe I got my point across."

Alana shows Dan to his room and tells him to get dressed for a swim. Mesa has dabbled with bodybuilding and has an excellent physique. He has wondered what Alana looks like in a bathing suit, but what he sees is more than he bargained for. She is absolutely gorgeous.

She sees Dan and says, "You are well built for an old guy. As a matter of fact, you could compete. Dan, you have a great body."

"Thank you, ma'am, I appreciate it. You are absolutely beautiful. I knew you would be gorgeous, but you surpass anything I could dream up. I hope you don't mind my staring at you, but you remind of a picture I saw in *Playboy* many years ago. I am amazed that some guy hasn't proposed to you."

"Several have asked me to marry them. However, they weren't my knight in shining armor. I have always had a picture in my mind of the right man for me. He would be the strong, loving type who would respect me for who I am and be willing to allow me to be a part his life and allow himself to be a part of mine. I want a man who is sure of himself, who is honest and God fearing and who wants to be my best friend. I am willing to follow him anyplace."

Dan Mesa listens and wonders why it has taken him so long to find such a person. He knows this lady is for him. However, because of past experiences he is afraid of committing himself to anyone. He decides to just wait and proceed cautiously. He has a feeling inside that is foreign to him.

Alana looks into his eyes and smiles while saying, "Ranger, I have your number and you know it. So let's swim. I know you don't like water much, although you never told me that. I know because you are my father reincarnated. So we will just enjoy the sun and the water."

"Alana, let's go dancing someplace where they play 'cowboy music' and the beer is cold and the atmosphere is friendly and warm. I must tell you that the last time I went dancing, it ended in a gunfight. Jackson hired a man to kill me, but he wasn't up to the task. So if you think I am bad luck, now is the time to get off the merry-go-round. I have been involved in six shootings in the last month. Two of those were fatalities. Alana, I haven't ever gone searching for trouble. Trouble has a way of finding me. You are a Ranger and you know my reputation. If you are the least bit apprehensive about getting involved with me, then now is the time to say something."

"Ranger, you do have a reputation. I have heard of you for the last two years."

"Alana, if you don't mind, would you tell me what they are saying about me?"

"Dan, most people don't know much about you, so they create stories. It is said that you are a throwback to the Rangers of the old days. You are supposed to be mean and hard as nails, with no give to you. Others say you are a rare breed of man, one to ride the river with. But mostly they say you are a good friend and a terrible enemy. All say you are honest and fair. Most of the women like you but don't understand you. You come across as being a loner and one of the saddest and most alone men I have ever met—at least that is what I thought before I came to know you. Now I know that you are one of the sweetest and most caring people I have ever met. You present a rough exterior, but inside where no one sees, there is a lot of hurt and pain you don't share with anyone."

Suddenly Dan feels a chill as if someone has walked across his grave.

In Durango, José Gutierrez-Jackson and Frank Stillwell are deep in planning. Stillwell wants to make a run for the border and argues with Jackson. "José, don't you realize this is not going to end the way you want it to? If Mesa is the sort of man you say he is, don't you think he will be after you everywhere you go? I have been hearing about him for the past five years, and what I have heard makes me worry about my life. Ranger Mesa spells trouble with a capital *T.* Personally, I don't want any part of Ranger Dan Mesa. José, you will be wise to give him a wide berth. He will be your death."

"Amigo, no one leaves this world alive. If I go out, I will go out with a bang, and if anyone gets in my way, so will they. I do regret starting all of this. Dan was the best friend a guy could have. We cut a trail from Texas to Arizona and back. We had a lot of fun in the process. Dan is the kind of guy who would lay down his life for a friend and has on several occasions. I would not be living today were it not for Mesa. I will regret killing him."

"José, have you considered the possibility that Mesa may kill you? You forget, I have seen both of you in action, and I can tell he is deadly in any kind of fight. José, if you challenge him, you will lose. I am telling you this because you are my friend. I got into a fight with Mesa about two years ago and he came close to killing me. I went after him with a knife and all he used was his necktie. He took it off and used it as if it were a rope. When I attacked, he caught my wrist with the tie and tripped me up. I went after him a second time and wound up with his tie around my throat, with him choking me. I never even scratched him, and he wasn't even breathing hard. José, he doesn't use karate or judo. He uses something I haven't heard of before. When he turned me loose, I hit him with everything I had, and you know I can punch. I knocked him down, but the only thing I accomplished was to make him angry. He got up and literally dusted himself off and walked right up to me and hit me in the stomach, and when I bent over, he hit me with an uppercut that knocked me off my feet. I got up and he just kicked me in the testicles. I passed out at that point. When I came to my senses, I was sitting in a chair in the bar with a drink in front of me with a note that read, "You have two choices: drink the drink and we will forget everything, or come after me and I will hurt you worse. The choice is yours." Well, I chose to drink the drink because I knew he would have killed me. I saw it in his eyes when he kicked me. José, I tell you, it was like looking into the face of hell itself. I did not only the right thing but the wise thing."

Jackson listens to what Stillwell is saying and knows he is right, but his pride will not allow him to admit it. He turns to Frank and says, "Just because you couldn't whip him doesn't mean that I can't. Dan never saw the day he could beat me in anything he attempted. I am better than he is. I at least got a bullet into him."Frank Stillwell becomes aware that Jackson has changed his entire demeanor in only a few minutes. Jackson's behavior is reminiscent of a caged tiger. He is nervous, and Stillwell sees the fear in his eyes, but he also sees something else and that is death. Frank Stillwell, the great-great-grandson of the original Frank Stillwell, becomes aware that he is headed for the same fate as his great-great-grandfather.

"Yes, José, you did get a bullet in him, but did you ever consider that the only reason you did was because he trusted you and you cheated?"

José turns quickly, with his hands poised to draw, and Frank Stillwell simply says, "José, don't ever draw on me, because I will kill you one way or another. You may get a bullet into me, but I will kill you with my last breath. I like you and we have been through a lot together, but that will not stop me from killing you."

Jackson suddenly realizes that he is slowly losing all his friends and that he can't afford to lose Frank Stillwell. Next to Mesa, Frank is his oldest friend. He drops his hands and relaxes, only to say to Frank, "I am sorry, man, but I sometimes take myself too seriously. I have lost one good friend, and I can't afford to lose another."

Frank Stillwell is no one's fool. With careful calculations he measures José closely and says, "José, I love you like a brother, but from this point on I will not trust you. I will hang in there with you, but don't ever attempt to draw on me again. It makes me think you are considering killing me, and that is something I would not like."

"Come on, Frank, that was just a knee-jerk reaction. I would never try to kill you!"

"Okay, José, let's forget it. What are our plans at this point? I know the Colorado State Police are watching us and just waiting for Mesa to arrive. I believe we should head south to New Mexico and slip across the border. I know someplace we can hide out."

Jackson, listening to Stillwell, knows that he should do as Frank suggests, but he also knows that it is only a matter of time before Ranger Mesa catches up to him. He wants it on his terms and he wants to determine the place. He knows his time is running out and that Mesa will have no mercy on him or anyone with him. He starts formulating a plan. "Frank, how good are you with a rifle?"

"I am good with any kind of weapon," Frank replies.

José continues, "I plan to take the attack to Ranger Dan Mesa. When he gets here, I plan to attack without warning and end this thing once and forever. I am tired of being chased like a fox."

In Nogales Captain Johnson is talking to Ranger Savalas. "Corporal Savalas, Sergeant Mesa was wearing a vest, wasn't he, when he was shot? So tell me, how was he injured?

"Captain, I looked at that vest when I pulled it off Sergeant Mesa and it had a bullet hole in it. Jackson was using Teflon-coated bullets, which they are illegal. I am not sure Dan knows about this either. Things were moving so fast that I forgot to mention it to him. So what do we do about this?"

Captain Johnson ponders for a moment and says, "Wait a minute! Dan is in Yuma, so I'll call Major McMasters."

"Major McMasters, Sam Johnson here."

"Hello, Sam, what can I do for you?"

"Major, when Sergeant Mesa was shot, he was wearing body armor, but the bullet still pierced the vest. It was because Jackson was using Teflon-coated bullets. Please inform Dan and all of your people. Also, if possible send a message to Durango and inform the police there about what they are possibly facing."

Major McMasters uses an expletive and says, "Sam, this Jackson character is really something. Where did he get those bullets? That bastard is really getting on my nerves. I am sending Lieutenant Osborne with Sergeant Mesa to Durango, so I'd better inform them right away. Sam, Alana and Dan would make a great couple. I know it's none of my business, but Sergeant Mesa seems to be a man in need of a significant other, and Alana is such a great person and a damned good Ranger. I just think they would be good for each other."

"Well, Major, I don't know the lieutenant that well, but from what I have been able to gather from talking to her on the phone, I must agree with you. So, I propose that you and I enter into a conspiracy and play Cupid. We will play them like a chessboard and move them together and hope to God we don't mess things up. What do you think?"

"Sam, it sounds like a plan. I will brief Alana and Dan about the bullets and get them started to Durango. Take care, Sam."

Captain Johnson turns to Savalas and says, "McMasters will brief the sergeant. Corporal, you heard that exchange between the major and me, so tell me what you think."

Savalas usually refrains from giving advice but says, "Captain, I met the lieutenant and she is very nice and very competent as a Ranger.

She asked me about the sergeant and I do believe she is interested in him in ways not consistent with Ranger work, if you get my meaning. I believe they should be together, but if you wait for Dan Mesa to make a move, you and I will be old men. He lives by a set of rules that don't allow for much socializing. He is a good man and a good friend. I wish I could help him find happiness. I worry about him. I know his temper and what drives him.

"Mike, we'll just have to wait and see how things progress."

In Yuma, Major McMasters is talking with Osborne and Mesa on the phone. "Sergeant, your captain called and asked me to inform you and my people that Jackson is using Teflon-coated bullets, which is why your body armor failed. I want all of you to be aware of what he is using. Don't take any unnecessary chances. Lieutenant, you and the sergeant had better get on the road sometime Sunday. Stay in touch. Sergeant, you are temporarily assigned to the Yuma detachment."

Lieutenant Osborne says, "Thanks for calling, sir. We will fly out on Sunday morning, and I will call you when we leave."

The lieutenant turns around and leads Dan into the bedroom, where she disrobes, and for a few minutes Dan Mesa remembers what it feels like to be happy and loved again. He sees a woman who knows how desirable she is and someone who is real and honest about her feelings. Is it possible that happiness could be just over the horizon for Sergeant Daniel Mesa?

There are some women in this world who have to work at being beautiful, and then there are those who are just naturally beautiful. Alana Osborne falls into the latter category. There is something about a stocking-clad leg that does wonders for the psyche.

Alana watches Dan as he sleeps and becomes aware of the turmoil he faces daily. He talks in his sleep and sometimes screams out about not wanting to shoot someone. Suddenly, he is awake and ready for "fight or flight."

"Dan, all is well. There isn't anything to worry about!"

He slowly becomes aware of where he is and makes the adjustment. He says, "Thanks for being here. I guess I talked in my sleep. I hope I didn't frighten you. I have a tendency to do that when I am in a strange bed. I don't mean that in the wrong way. I just meant that when I sleep in a strange place, I have problems sleeping."

Alana looks at him with a smile and says, "Dan I know what you meant and you don't have to defend yourself. I was concerned about you because you seem to have been in distress about killing someone. Is it a recurring dream?"

"I sometimes have flashbacks to certain events in my life when I sleep. I must apologize for my behavior. I do enjoy being with you and I still want to take you dancing. Maybe we can dance this dance again tonight."

Alana smiles and says, "If you are a very nice man, you may get your wish later on tonight. Now, let's take a bath and get ready for tonight. You may take yours here in the guest bedroom, or we can take one together."

"My dear lady. it will be my pleasure to soap you down and rinse you off."

Dan Mesa, while dressing, begins to reflect on his life, his loves, and his losses. His mind drifts back to Sonia as always, and there are still pains associated with her memory. He wishes things were different and that somehow she was still a part of his life. He feels guilty not being with her.

Meanwhile, back in Amado, Sonia isn't her normal self. Mesha has been watching her and finally says, "Sonia, you are my dearest friend and I love you as a sister, so I feel obligated to say that you are slowly falling apart. I know you love that Ranger and he surely does love you. I watched him drive away with a rejected look in his eyes. The way he looked said more than words. He has been rejected before and something terrible has happened to him. The two of you belong together. Somehow or another you must get back together. It is the only way you will ever get yourself together again. What do you plan to do about yourself?"

Sonia answers in a tearful voice, "I don't know what to do with myself. All I can manage to do is work and cry. I know he is somewhere thinking of me because I can feel his thoughts right at this moment. It's as if we are connected in some way. I know I have made a terrible mistake, and maybe someday I will get a chance to correct it. For now I will have to live with my decision, however difficult it is. Some days I manage to make it through without breaking down. I wish I had handled this situation differently. Every time I hear a gunshot, it reminds me of what happened to my husband, Pepe, and I fall apart all over again. Mesha, I am glad you are here with me, because I am not so sure I could handle this right now. Thanks for being a good friend."

"No thanks is needed. I know you would do the same for me. We'll make it through this."Yuma, Arizona, is one of the hottest places in the state. But nighttime in the desert can be deceiving, and tonight is no exception. It is always appropriate to carry a jacket at night while in the desert. Dan Mesa, being a cautious man, dresses appropriately in gray pants, powder blue shirt, burgundy tie, dark blue sports jacket, and black boots. The last item he adds is a .45 automatic in a shoulder holster. To Mesa, a gun is simply another item of clothing, essential to his dress.

Alana has chosen a pants suit that accentuates her figure to the point that she is wondering if Dan will think she is being too coy. She decides to forgo the pants suit in favor of a silk hunter-green dress with an elongated waist with a sash belt. The dress makes her look ten years younger.

Dan is standing on the back patio looking at the horses grazing when Alana takes his arm. He turns and what he sees takes his breath away. He stammers and finally says, "Alana, you are absolutely gorgeous. I thank you for choosing to like me and to allow me to take you to dinner."

Alana Osborne is a woman who knows how to accept a compliment. She immediately puts her arms around Dan and kisses him tenderly on the cheek and watches him blush. To which she says, "Now I know why I love you the way I do. It is because under that hard exterior is a very lovable guy who needs to be loved and reminded that he is human and that there is one woman who finds him extremely handsome and caring."

They decide to take her father's old '56 Mercury classic and go to dinner and dancing. Alana suddenly asks, "Dan, do you have your service revolver with you?"

"Yes, I always carry it. Why do you ask?"

Alana says, "Because I don't want anything to happen to you. From what you told me, someone has tried to kill you three times and I don't want them to succeed."

Yuma has its share of nightclubs and restaurants. On this night the Holiday Inn has the country group Asleep at the Wheel in concert. It is a dinner and dance occasion. Yuma's temperature apparently has an effect on its people. It makes them crazy, and they do things they regret. Tonight is no exception. As Mesa and Osborne arrive— a man and woman are arguing in the lobby. As the Rangers approach, the two individuals draw their weapons and fire. Dan and Alana fire back, hitting both of them. The man attempts to shoot Mesa and

Alana yells, *"NO!"* She jumps in front of Mesa, taking a bullet to the head. Dan Mesa turns and empties his weapon into the individuals, shooting them to pieces. He runs to Alana.

"Someone, please call an ambulance. She has been shot."

A man in a black suit approaches and says, "I am a doctor. Can I help?"

He examines Lieutenant Osborne and says, "She is badly injured. The bullet grazed her and she apparently hit her head when she fell. I'd say she is in a coma right now. We have to get her to the hospital." Dan covers her with his coat and slowly sits down next to her, unable to believe what has happened. The male gunman says, "José warned me that you were good. I shouldn't have gotten involved." He suddenly spasms and dies.

Everyone present hears his remarks, including the mayor of Yuma, who happens to be close by. The ambulance arrives and Ranger Osborne is rushed to the hospital with Mesa riding shotgun. Dan remembers and notifies Major McMasters and Alana's mother.

The scene at the hospital is dramatic. A beautiful woman arrives with a gunshot to the head wearing a beautiful evening dress, accompanied by a gentleman covered in blood and wearing a gun and a Ranger shield. He is consumed with anger, and yet the way he takes her hand indicates there is something special between them.

Major McMasters arrives along with Adelaide, Alana's mother. Dan meets them and slowly falls apart. He explains what happened and how Alana took a bullet meant for him.

McMasters asks, "How is she doing? What is her condition?"

Dan answers, saying, "They took her into emergency and then told me to wait out here and they'd tell her condition as soon as they could stop the bleeding. It has been an hour. She was shot in the head, but the bullet only grazed her. When she fell, she hit her head on a table or a chair. I didn't see everything because of the shooting. When I turned around, Alana was lying on the floor. She took a bullet meant for me. According to one of the assailants, José Gutierrez-Jackson sent them. Their comments were witnessed by the mayor and several politicians."

"Excuse me, I am Dr. Wainwright, chief of surgery. Miss Osborne is in serious condition. She suffered a trauma to the brain caused by the grazing bullet and the blow she received as she fell. The problem we face is the brain swelling. We have to reduce the swelling. A point in our favor is that she is in a coma. On the other hand, the coma could last a day, a month, a year, or several years." He looks at Adelaide and says, "I assume you are her mother. Mrs. Osborne, I suggest you stay the night with her. The others of you should go home and get some rest. Ranger Mesa, I think you need a sedative, because you look as if you are about to explode. I mean no disrespect, sir, but it appears as if you are ready to fall apart. Go home and change clothes and come back. I have an extra room and you can stay the night."

"Thank you, doctor. I believe I will do as you say. I must report this to—"

Sergeant Dan Mesa suddenly collapses. Major McMasters grabs him before he hits the floor. Dr. Wainwright quickly examines him and says, "He is suffering from the shock of what has happened. He will be okay physically; however, mentally, I'd say he will need observing. Let's put him to bed here in the hospital. Major, it appears you have two people here who are something special."

Adelaide Matilda Osborne suddenly feels the weight of the world on her shoulders. It brings back the death of her husband, and she slowly cries and prays: "God, please save these two. I love them both dearly, and I beg you to spare them." She prays a simple prayer, from the heart of a person who believes deeply.

The phone rings at the home of Colonel Grant. "Sir, Major McMasters here. I regret to tell you that one of my Rangers, Lieutenant Alana Osborne, was shot tonight and is in a coma in the hospital. She and Sergeant Mesa were attending a dance at the Holiday Inn, when a man and a woman opened fire on them. Alana received a head wound from a bullet and also a blow to the head when she fell. Colonel, she stepped in front of a bullet meant for Sergeant Mesa."

"Major, what is the condition of Lieutenant Osborne and Sergeant Mesa?" The colonel's voice is strained and angered.

"Sir, Lieutenant Osborne is in serious condition. According to the doctor, her brain is swelling because of the pressure on it. He says it is good that she is in the coma. It allows them to treat her without the stress of her being conscious. The bad news is she could be in a coma for a long time. Sergeant Mesa wasn't wounded, but I believe that the stress of what happened to Alana and what has happened to him in the past few weeks caused him to collapse. I believe he will be okay physically, but mentally, sir, he will be ten times as dangerous. Please notify Captain Johnson. Sir, witnesses say one of the assailants said Jackson sent them."

"Major, where are these would-be assassins?"

"Colonel, Mesa killed both of them. He shot them to pieces. Sir, Dan and Alana were serious about each other and this will not settle well with him. Also, Mesa has killed four people in the last three weeks, all in the line of duty and all associated with Jackson. Sir, what do we do now?"

Colonel Grant says, in a voice that sounds like thunder, "We turn Mesa loose and let him do what he does so well, and we protect him when it is all over. Do you understand me?"

Major McMasters understands exactly what the colonel means and says in return, "Yes, sir, I understand and agree. I will ensure nothing happens to Dan Mesa. Colonel, when this is over, please let him have some time off to get himself together."

Meanwhile, the newspaper television and radio have arrived on the scene and are broadcasting the story. Channel 11 KYUMA has broken in on the local programs to report the news. "This is Jim Roberts of Channel 11 news reporting from the Holiday Inn here in Yuma, where a shooting has taken place. Apparently two gunmen attempted to kill two of our Rangers, Lieutenant Alana Osborne and Sergeant Dan Mesa. Osborne was shot but is alive and in serious condition in the Catholic hospital here in Yuma. Mesa returned fire and killed both suspects. Sergeant Mesa is from the Santa Cruz Company and has been involved in three previous shootings that ended in the death of the people involved. Witnesses say José Gutierrez-Jackson sent the gunmen. Gutierrez-Jackson is accused of robbing an armored truck and killing four people in the past few weeks. Although Rangers have been chasing him for the last month or so, they haven't yet caught him. This is Jim Roberts with Channel 11 news, on the scene in Yuma." In Amado, Sonia is listening to the television news and learns of Dan's involvement in yet another shooting. She has told herself a thousand times these last few days that no matter what happens, she is going to make sure Dan knows how much she loves him, yet upon hearing of this latest shooting, she finds herself rejecting the thought of him killing another human.

Mesha walks in saying, "Sonia, did you hear about the shooting Dan was involved in? Apparently a man and a woman tried to kill him and another Ranger. The female Ranger was badly injured and Dan killed both of the gunmen. He is in the hospital also but no one is saying why. Girl, what is wrong with you? Why are you crying?"

"Mesha, I have tried to accept Dan's way of life but I just can't! It is too violent. He has been involved in at least four shootings since I have known him. He has been shot at three times and shot once, and now another Ranger is in the hospital because of him. It is more than a body can take."

Mesha walks over and puts an arm around her shoulders to comfort her. But what can one do under the circumstances other than be a friend?

In Durango, José learns of the failure of his hired gunmen. He realizes he made a terrible mistake. The phone rings and he answers. "Hello, Dad. How are you and Mom doing?"

"José, you have been a bad boy again. Those two people you sent to kill Daniel Mesa talked, and he knows you sent them. Son, I have a bad feeling you have signed your death warrant. Daniel will be looking for you, and this time no one can help you. José, you should go for cover. Go to Mexico and hide out there. Your life is over if you stay in Durango or anyplace in this country. José, Mesa is coming for you, so run!"

"Papa, I have really messed things up. I know him and yes, he will kill me now. I am now afraid of him, because this will turn him into an animal and when he is like that, nothing short of God will stop him. I am going to pack up and run, so good-bye and give Momma a hug for me."

Frank Stillwell walks in and José looks at him and says, "Don't say it. Yes, I was a fool, but I had already hired them before we spoke earlier. I really messed things up this time. One of them talked before they died and named me, according to the news. I am going to make a run for it for Mexico. Do you want to come with me?"

"José, sometimes I wonder about you. You are my buddy, so I guess I am in it all the way. However, I don't think we are going to survive this one. If Mesa is the kind of man I believe he is, he will shoot us and ask no questions. About now he is mad-dog angry and getting meaner by the minute. You do know the police are aware we are here, right? I recommend we light a shuck for Mexico right now."

In their rush to pack, José leaves a map by mistake with markings about their route. As they walk out of their room, the Colorado State Police are arriving. Frank is getting into the truck when the police open fire, wounding him. José pushes him out of the truck and speeds off in a hail of bullets.Stillwell is taken to the local hospital to be treated for his wounds. He has a bullet in his back close to his spine and another in his chest close to the heart. Either wound could kill him. He asks the doctor to take his statement in which he says that José is making a run for Mexico through Albuquerque. He says, "Please tell Ranger Mesa I am sorry about what happened to him and the lady. I didn't have any part in that. I am so, so—." He gasps and dies. So ends the life of another Stillwell.

The police search the motel room used by Jackson and Stillwell and find the map and other valuable information. A call is placed to Yuma to the Rangers' office.

"Arizona Rangers, Sergeant Valdez speaking."

"Sergeant Valdez, this is Lieutenant Ben Grimm of the Colorado State Police in Durango. We had a run-in with José Gutierrez-Jackson and Frank Stillwell. Jackson got away, but Stillwell was wounded and later died. He did give us some valuable information, and I am faxing it to you. We heard about Rangers Mesa and Osborne, and all of us send our best wishes."

"Thank you, Lieutenant, I will pass it on to the major. Sergeant Mesa is okay, but Lieutenant Osborne is in a coma and we just don't know about her condition. I'll be waiting on your fax."

It is now 11:30 p.m. and the watch at the hospital continues. Adelaide Osborne is sitting holding Alana's hand when Dan walks in. Adelaide looks at him and sees tears in his eyes. In voice heavy with sorrow he says to her, "I am so sorry about what has happened. I never intended for Alana to get hurt. It seems as if everyone I care about gets hurt because of me. She is very, very special to me. I haven't ever met a person with a heart and soul like hers. I am going after Jackson and put an end to this, once and for all this time. Mrs. Osborne, you probably hate me for what has happened and I can't blame you, but know I love her deeply. I never got a chance to tell her how much she means to me. I will be back when this is over. Talk to her constantly and please tell her my spirit is here watching over her. I love you both very much."

He turns to leave when he hears Adelaide's voice. "Dan, this is not your fault. What happened here is the fault of one person, Jackson. Do me a favor and send him straight to hell! Dan, come back to us. We both need you. Think of that little fellow who lives in Virginia. He needs you also. Be careful and don't take any unnecessary chances. You live for yourself and your beliefs; let Jackson die for his deeds and beliefs."

Ranger Dan Mesa walks slowly away, never looking back. He decides not to stay at the hospital and takes a cab back to the Holiday Inn and collects Alana's car. He takes it back to her house, where he collects his truck along with some heavy firepower. He then goes to the Rangers' office.

Sergeant Valdez sees him as he enters and says, "Sergeant Mesa, are you all right? How is the lieutenant?"

"Sergeant, she isn't doing well at all. She is still in a coma, and I just don't know what to think. Have you heard anything about Jackson?"

"Yes, we got a fax from Durango and the state police. They got into a shootout with Jackson and Frank Stillwell. Stillwell was killed but Jackson escaped. He left a map behind, which shows where he is headed. Stillwell made a statement and told them where Jackson is headed and said to tell you that the attempted assassination was not his doing, only Jackson's. What do you plan to do now?"

"I am going after Jackson. Can I have a copy of the map and can I use one of the four-by-fours? My 4Runner wouldn't stand up to what I need to do. Tell Major McMasters I will be in touch."

"Dan, you be careful and stay alive. The major puts high value on you and the lieutenant. He has this idea that the two of you should be together. I don't know you well, but you measure up to being a straight shooter, so you are aces in my book."

Ranger Mesa nods and walks away.

Somewhere on Interstate 25 heading south, José assesses his life and reaches the conclusion that he has lost all of his friends and that his family has distanced themselves from him. Suddenly, José Gutierrez-Jackson finds himself very much alone. He wonders to himself how his life got so far off track. He remembers a time when he and Dan Mesa were inseparable. If one had a dollar, the other did also. They were closer than brothers. He drives on and on, knowing that death is only a few hundred miles behind him. He knows his life is almost over on this earth. "Dan, if I could only turn back the hands of time, I would do things differently." It is now six o'clock on Sunday morning and he is in Santa Fe headed south. He stops for gas and goes into the store for a Coke. His face is on the TV screen and the news announcer is saying, "If you see this man, do not attempt to apprehend him. Call your local law enforcement officer. Be advised he is armed and very dangerous. He is suspected of killing at least four members of law enforcement. He has also been implicated in the attempted assassination of two Arizona Rangers last evening in Yuma, Arizona. Jackson has vowed not to be taken alive. Ranger Lieutenant Alana Osborne lies in a coma in the Catholic hospital in Yuma, and Ranger Dan Mesa is in pursuit of Jackson. We haven't spoken with Ranger Mesa yet He has the reputation of a person who never quits.. We at KRTQ Channel 6 wish the Ranger good luck in apprehending this individual. This is Susan McBebe, Channel 6 News."

Jackson pays for his purchases and walks away, never looking back. He gets into his truck and drives away. He knows it is time to get rid of the truck. He continues to drive, looking for a chance to steal another vehicle. He sees a Dodge dealership and pulls off the road. It is early and no one is about. He chooses a silver Dodge four-by-four diesel and changes the tags. He uses a "jimmy" to unlock the doors and hot-wires the switch. He suddenly notices the lock box on the window. He squirts acid into the lock and opens the lock. He takes the keys and drives away in another vehicle, hoping it will buy him enough time to get away. He pulls onto the interstate and continues driving south.

Back in Yuma, Major McMasters asks, "Sergeant Valdez, where is Sergeant Mesa?"

"Major, he came in and asked for all information we had recently received on Jackson, so I gave him a copy of the FAX from Durango. He asked to borrow one of the four-by-fours and then he left. Is there a problem? He said to tell you he will check in with you later."

"No, Sergeant, there isn't a problem. I am just worried about what he will do when he catches up to Jackson. Mesa isn't your average Ranger. He is something different. Something drives him. He spent time in Vietnam and the Persian Gulf and probably places we haven't ever heard of. Rumor has it he was involved in the evacuation of Saigon when the Vietcong were approaching to take over back in '75. Supposedly he had to kill a few Vietcong and some South Vietnamese soldiers. The South Vietnamese soldiers were raping a young girl. He killed two and castrated the others. During the Gulf

War, he was almost blown up twice. Since he has been a Ranger, he has cut a wide path through the criminal community. They hate him, but they respect him because he is a man of his word and treats everyone—man or woman, criminal or innocent—the same and with respect. It is said he arrested a guy once for burglary and that when he found out that the man's family was in need, he used his own money and purchased food and paid the rent and utilities until the wife found a job and got on her feet. He is one person I would not want to have after me."

Sergeant Valdez listens and asks, "Major, how will all of this end?"

Major McMasters shakes his head and says, "Sergeant, I haven't a clue. I pray that Mesa catches Jackson and returns him to stand trial. But knowing the criminal mind, Jackson will not be taken alive. Dan will have to kill him. Jackson is tough, but he is running scared. He has tried to kill Mesa four times, and each time, Mesa survived. Jackson is afraid, and he is making mistakes. Dan Mesa will not make mistakes."

In Amado Sonia is wide awake, her eyes red from crying. Mesha is sleeping of the couch. At the hospital in Yuma, Adelaide is watching her only child breathing and wondering whether she will survive this.

The editorial in the Tucson paper reads as follows:
"Sergeant Daniel Mesa of the Arizona Rangers has killed two more people. Doesn't he know the days of the gunslingers are over? Ranger Mesa recently was involved in a shooting at Clancy's here in Tucson, where an individual was shot and killed. In Yuma, he was involved in another shooting where people were killed also. Last night he shot and killed two people who were attempting to kill him and another Ranger. It is reported that Ranger Mesa killed these two people on the spot. We have estimated that within the last four weeks Ranger Mesa has gunned down four people. We believe it is time for Ranger Mesa to hang up his 'shooting irons' and disappear."

In Nogales, Captain Johnson is reading the paper and is so angry he sees red. He dials the colonel's home and says, "Sir, have you seen today's paper? It is total garbage. That paper has about as much integrity as a rattlesnake."

"Calm down, Sam. I've seen the paper, and no one with any common sense believes that stuff. I use those editorials to line the birdcage on the balcony. Now, we must ensure that we put out the true story of all of this. The governor is on our side. All of the politicians want Jackson captured. The shooting of Lieutenant Osborne bought us a lot of sympathy from the right people. She is well respected and so was her father. If she survives this, we must make sure she is adequately rewarded and given time off. As for Dan, I don't know what to do for him. Just let him recover and keep a watch on him. Send him to see his son for a while, or better yet keep him close so that he is around friends. If the lieutenant doesn't survive her injuries, Dan Mesa could become a handful. Sam, keep a watch over him. He is a very good man with nowhere to go and no one to go to. Anyway, keep me posted."

Captain Johnson hangs up the phone and wonders what to do about his friend and fellow Ranger. He picks up the phone and calls Sonia. The phone rings at Sonia's place. "This is Sonia Perdenales."

"Sonia, Captain Johnson from the Rangers. I am sure you have been watching television and seen the news about the shooting Dan was involved in, in Yuma."

"Yes, Captain, I've seen the news."

"Sonia, Dan told me how you felt about the previous shootings he was involved in. I want you to know that this was not of his choosing. Each time it was forced upon him. This latest shooting was another case in point. The assailants were sent to kill him and Lieutenant Osborne, who took a bullet for him. Sergeant Mesa is as fine a man as ever walked God's green earth. However, this latest shooting could take its toll on him. You are letting a very good man get away. He is my friend and I want him to be happy. He has paid some high prices for serving his country and his fellow man. Sergeant Mesa and all of the Rangers risk their lives every day for others and never receive any rewards. How much must they sacrifice before it is enough?"

In a voice filled with emotion, Sonia says, "Captain, I don't know what to do. I sat at my husband's bedside and watched him die from a gunshot wound, and all I could do was pray and cry. I promised myself I would never go through that again. When I met Dan, I never thought things would end up this way. I feel as if my heart will explode and I don't know what to do. I care about him, more than you can imagine, but maybe not enough to risk seeing him killed."

"Sonia, I understand. I may not agree with you, but I understand. Sometimes you have to just go for it and pray and hope for the best. I can't tell you what to do. Only you know what is best for you. Do what you think is best. However, remember life offers no guarantees. If you are to be happy, you have to take risks sometimes. If you need someone to talk with, I am here. Take care. Bye."

Somewhere, just west of Albuquerque, Ranger Dan Mesa is traveling east on Interstate 40 when he sees a New Mexico state trooper signaling for him to pull over. He guides the truck to the side of the road and kills the engine.

"Hello, Ranger, I am Sergeant Morales of the New Mexico State Police. I know you guys are looking for José Gutierrez-Jackson, and he is supposed to be driving a maroon Dodge Durango with an eagle painted on the hood. Ranger, I believe I saw Jackson earlier today driving a silver-colored Dodge truck four-by-four. The license number was Arizona 374 ALL. I gave chase but lost him in Gallup. I have been searching for him since. He is probably headed for Albuquerque."Ranger Mesa is surprised at the help he is receiving from police along the way. He says, "Thank you, Sergeant, for the information. I have been chasing Jackson for about a month now. I've gotten close but not close enough."

The sergeant looks down and says, "Ranger Mesa, we heard about what happened to you and the lieutenant, and I just want to say I'm sorry about that. I lost a partner under similar circumstances, and it will take you some time to get over it. If I or any of the department can help, give us a call."

"Thank you, Sergeant. I may have to do that. Tell everyone in the department thanks for me. So long."

Dan has been thinking of Alana. His heart is heavy, and the anger and hatred are consuming him. He puts in a CD by Patsy Cline and plays "Crazy," and the tears fall. He is relieved that no one is around to see a tough, battle-hardened Ranger cry. The song ends and he changes tapes, this time playing a Willie Nelson tape, "Borderline." He continues driving east.

In Albuquerque, José finds Central Avenue and stops at a Best Western. He signs in using the name Frank Mesa. He thinks to himself, "Dan would get a kick out of this." He suddenly remembers that Dan Mesa is no longer a friend. His heart suddenly skips a beat and he almost falls. The night clerk sees him and rushes to his aid. She says, "Sir, are you all right?"

José looks at her and says, "No, ma'am, I'm not okay and haven't been for a while. But not to worry: I will survive, thanks for asking. It has been a long time since anyone cared enough to ask." He walks to his room with bag in hand, another lost soul.

The clerk walks back to the counter and looks at the name Frank Mesa. There is something strange about the name and the man, but she can't put it all together. She leaves a memo for the day clerk. She checks her watch. It is 11:55 p.m., and her shift ends at midnight. She turns the keys over to the next clerk and heads home.

After arriving home she turns on the TV. The news is on and the reporter is talking about a shooting in Yuma and someone named José Gutierrez-Jackson. She misses the photo. She gets ready for bed.Dan Mesa arrives in Albuquerque and checks in with the state police. He walks into the station and approaches the desk sergeant.

"Good morning, I'm Sergeant Mesa of the Arizona Rangers, and I am in pursuit of one José Gutierrez-Jackson, who is wanted for bank robbery, murder, attempted murder, and a few other charges added in."

The desk sergeant looks up and says, "I'll be damned, it is you! Please, come in and I will get the lieutenant." The sergeant returns with a lieutenant. "Ranger Mesa, I am Lieutenant Jamison. Your boss, a Major McMasters, called and asked us to be on the watch for you. He told us what happened and we are sorry. We have had our guys on the watch for Jackson but so far nothing. Why not get a hotel room. Let us know where you are and we'll call you if anything comes down."

"Thanks, Lieutenant. Can you recommend a hotel and a restaurant?"

The lieutenant says, "Sure, there is a Ramada Inn right down the street and there is a Waffle House right next to it."

"Thanks, sir, and thank you, sergeant." Mesa turns and walks away, shoulders straight and never a smile.

Lieutenant Jackson turns to Sergeant Laughlin and says, "Did you notice how he never smiled and his eyes were like hot steel burning into your soul? That man is dangerous and I wouldn't want him after me. Rumor has it he is one of the best they have in Arizona. Something is driving that man. Jackson did something to him, and whatever it was must have been bad. I can read people and Ranger Mesa is one angry man."

Mesa pulls into the parking lot of the Waffle House and goes in. As he opens the door, the news is on and the reporter is talking about the Yuma shooting. "This is Ted Koppel with *Nightline,* and now the news. In Yuma, Arizona, there was a shooting involving the Arizona Rangers. Apparently, it was a contract shooting to kill one of the Rangers, a Sergeant Daniel Mesa. Mesa has been chasing a wanted criminal, José Gutierrez-Jackson, for armed robbery and murder. Jackson is suspected of hiring two people to kill Ranger Mesa, but in the attempt, Lieutenant Alana Osborne, another Ranger, was shot and is in the hospital in serious condition. Ranger Mesa is unavailable for comment." A picture of Dan Mesa is shown along with a photo of Jackson.

Mesa walks in and takes a seat, hoping no one will say anything about the newscast. The waitress walks over and looks at him and the badge and says, "You are the Ranger I just saw on TV, aren't you?"

Dan nods and says yes. The waitress continues talking and says, "What can I get for you?"

Mesa orders scrambled eggs, bacon, wheat toast, sliced tomatoes, coffee, and juice. The waitress brings him coffee and all heads turn toward him and quickly turn away. He hears the undercurrent of conversations about him. A few minutes later the waitress returns with more coffee and says, "I heard over the news that another Ranger was shot. How is she doing?"

Mesa slowly answers, "She is in a coma and it doesn't look good at all. She doesn't deserve this. She is an outstanding Ranger and a great person." The waitress leaves and returns with his food, and he eats in silence.

In Yuma at the hospital, Adelaide is sitting by Alana's bed and praying when suddenly Alana awakens and looks around as if she is lost. "Mom, why am I here in the hospital?"
Adelaide calls for a nurse and says, "Sweetheart, don't you remember what happened? You were shot when you and Dan were at the Holiday Inn having dinner. Don't you remember?"

Alana says, "The last thing I remember is falling. Who is Dan?"

The doctor arrives along with the nurse. Adelaide is explaining what happened. "Alana, don't you remember Dan Mesa? He is the Ranger who came to us from Nogales and has been helping chase José Gutierrez-Jackson. You and he have become very close. I thought you two were in love. Honey, do you remember the gun battle in which he was injured, and the time the two of you spent together?"

The doctor breaks in and says, "Mrs. Osborne, she has temporary memory loss. It is not uncommon in cases like this. Usually, the memory returns after a few days. However, it may take a few months and even a year in some cases. Just let her rest and we will talk some more tomorrow."

"Mom, this Dan Mesa person, what kind of man is he?"

Adelaide explains. "Honey, he is something like your father, except he is, well, let me just say he is of African descent and from New Orleans. I believe he is referred to as being Creole. He is handsome, intelligent, and most of all a really nice person who cares a lot about both of us. He is in love with you and that I know for sure. He has been through a lot. He is out looking for Jackson now, and I am worried about him. After you were shot, we had to put him in the hospital overnight and the next morning, he looked in on you and left. He has gone after Jackson, and this time one of them will die."

117

Alana looks confused and says, "I don't remember any of that. It sounds as if he is something special because you seem to like him. If he is anything like Dad, then he must be okay. I think I'll go to sleep now."

Adelaide says a prayer of thanks and stretches out on her bed to get some sleep also.

In Albuquerque the motel clerk sees the news, picks up the phone, and calls the police. She tells them that a man bearing the likeness of Jackson has a room at the Best Western motel where she works. She says, "He registered as Frank Mesa, but he is Jackson."

Lieutenant Jackson calls all available patrolmen in and begins making plans. "Call Sergeant Mesa at the Waffle House and have him report back here. Do it now!"

Mesa's phone rings. "Sergeant Mesa here. Yes, I will leave right now." Dan pays the bill and leaves. He arrives at headquarters and is briefed.

The lieutenant tells everyone to put on their vest and says, "Let's roll, people. Sergeant Mesa, this is your case. What do you want to do?"

"Sir, Jackson is dangerous and very tricky. When we arrive, let me try to talk to him. He is dangerous because he is running out of time. He has tried to kill me four times and has failed each time. I will try to talk him into surrendering. If that doesn't work, I will try to get him to meet me man to man. If he will agree, then there is less chance of an innocent bystander getting hurt."

The lieutenant looks at Mesa and says, "Exactly what do you mean when you say 'man to man'?"

Mesa explains in detail. "Jackson has bragged that he will kill me because I am the only person alive who thinks as he does. He knows that I am just as good as he is with any weapon, and since we were once good friends, I know everything about him."

Sergeant Laughlin does a double take. "You were once friends with this maniac and now he wants to kill you? How did that happen?"

"Sergeant, somewhere along the way Jackson changed from being a very good person to a completely bad individual. I don't know when the change occurred, because for a while we weren't in touch. He spent time in the Peace Corps and in Africa. . He was involved in a shooting in Mexico over a girl, and then he spent time in prison for a crime he didn't commit and after that he changed. I often wish I had been around to keep him out of trouble, but I guess— Who knows?"

I could explain a lot to the sergeant, but what is the use? It is all pointless, because one of us will die now. I wish I could talk to Alana. I guess happiness for me is just not meant to be.

Lieutenant Jackson is saying, "Let's move, people. One last thing: be careful out there."

We have arrived at the motel. Now to try to get Jackson to come out. The phone rings in his room. Jackson answers, "Room twenty-six."

"José, Dan Mesa here. Look out your window!"

Jackson looks out the window and says, "How did you find me, and what do you want?"

"I want you to come outside with your hands up and no weapons. This is the end of the trail for you."

"Dan, it's not that simple, you see. I have placed a bomb in this motel and I can set it off anytime I want to. So, maybe it isn't over. Here is what I want. I want you to meet me one on one and we will settle all of this."

"José, why have you done the things you've done? This could have been avoided. What have I done to you for you to want me dead?"

He answers in an angry tone, "All I have heard for the last two years is Ranger Dan Mesa and what a great guy he is, and how fast you are, and how good you can fight. Well, prove it! Either you prove it or I will blow the building and everyone in it to hell!"

"José, the lady you shot was a personal friend of mine and she never did one thing to you, so why the assassination attempt?"

"Dan, I never wanted anything to happen to her. She took that bullet for you. This whole thing has gone to hell, so now you have a chance to end it. I plan to walk away, so you'd better be ready to kill me. What do you plan to do?"

"Okay, José, I will meet you in the parking lot, but when we meet, you must tell me where the bomb is. You have my word I will face you."

"Dan, I am coming out with my hands in the air. The bomb is in the generator room in a black canvas bag. I am coming out."

Mesa and Jackson meet in the parking lot of the motel. The police and bystanders are watching, and so is a TV crew. Both take off their weapons and a strange kind of dance begins. Jackson circles to the right and Mesa moves left on the balls of his feet. Suddenly Jackson rushes in and throws a left hook to Mesa's midsection, knocking him off his feet. Jackson throws a kick and Mesa rolls away and jumps up.

Mesa looks at Jackson, simply smiles a dead smile, and squared his shoulders. José fakes a left. Mesa blocks it, grabs his arm, and quickly flips him over his shoulder. Mesa sends a kick to Jackson's knee. As Jackson goes down again, Mesa hits him with an open hand chop, splitting his cheek and sending blood down his cheek.

Jackson curses, saying, "Now you have made me mad and I am going to hurt you for that." He swings a heavy right fist to Mesa's jaw. Mesa shakes it off and circles to the left. It becomes a slug-fest. Both men are battered.

Jackson rushes in and Mesa hits him with an uppercut, knocking Jackson completely off his feet. Mesa literally picks José up over his head and tosses him onto one of the police cars. Mesa turns away, walks over, and buckles on his pistol. Jackson dives for his gun and comes up shooting. Mesa simply draws his weapon and runs at Jackson, yelling and firing as he runs. Jackson takes a bullet in the chest and another in the stomach, and falls. He drops his gun and lies very still.

Dan walks closer, his gun poised to fire. José is breathing hard with blood running out of his mouth. "Dan, I am so sorry about all this. I just got myself in so deep and I couldn't stop. You are the best friend I ever had. I guess I—." He suddenly shudders and dies.

Lieutenant Jackson is terribly shaken. He can't believe what he has just seen. It was bloody! It was barbaric, and yet it was good triumphing over evil. He has something to tell his grandchildren. He walks over to Mesa, simply shakes his head, pats him on the shoulder, and guides him away from the cameras. A reporter asks, "Ranger, would you be willing to make a statement or sit for a simple interview to give your side of this?"

Dan looks at the reporter and says, "This is my statement. I have been chasing Jackson for just about a month. The state of Arizona wanted him for armed robbery of a Wells Fargo truck and killing the two guards. He is wanted for the killing of two police officers in Arizona also. He has tried to kill me on four different occasions. I have a partner who is fighting for her life in Yuma, so I believe under these circumstances we were justified in taking him off the streets."

"But Ranger, the manner in which he met his fate was somewhat drastic, wouldn't you say?"

"Yes, it was drastic but he had threatened to blow up the motel unless I met him in the street one on one. I could not risk the lives of the people in the motel. I get paid to risk my life, they don't. I did what was expected of me."

It is now three in the morning and Mesa is back at the police station. The bomb squad found the bomb and deactivated it. Dan is sitting in the lieutenant's office trying to compose himself. But how do you adjust to killing a man who used to be your best friend?

The TV is on when the news program *Daybreak* begins.

"Good morning, this is *Daybreak* in Albuquerque. Earlier this morning the fugitive José-Gutierrez-Jackson was cornered and killed at the Best Western motel on Central Avenue. It seems the Arizona Rangers have been chasing him for quite a while, and Ranger Dan Mesa caught up with him earlier this morning. Jackson threatened to blow up the motel unless Mesa met him in the streets for a fistfight. Mesa met him in the streets and soundly whipped Jackson in one of the most brutal fights I have ever seen. Mesa was battered and bruised in this fight with a man twice his size. The fight was over and Mesa was buckling on his gun when Jackson went for his gun. Mesa, in a shootout reminiscent of the Old West, drew his gun and killed Jackson, ending a crime spree covering Arizona, Colorado, and New Mexico. As a side note, I take my hat off to the Arizona Rangers, Texas Rangers, and all law enforcement agents everywhere for the work they do."

Lieutenant Jackson gets up and turns the TV off. He says to Mesa, "Sergeant, you look like you've been through hell. Why don't you go back to your room, take a bath, relax; get some sleep and come back in this afternoon? I'll call your boss and tell him what happened."

"Thanks, Lieutenant, I believe I will do just that." Mesa gets up and walks out of the office with a stiff gait.

At the Catholic hospital in Yuma, Dr. Wainwright rushes into Alana's room and turns on the TV. "You've got to see this!" he says. The announcer is saying, "In a situation reminiscent of the Wild West, the Albuquerque PD and a member of the Arizona Rangers shot and killed fugitive José Jackson-Gutierrez last night. Details are still sketchy, but from what we have pieced together, Jackson was cornered in a motel in Albuquerque. He demanded that the Ranger meet him in streets or he'd blow up the motel. Ranger Dan Mesa met him in the streets, and they fought, as you can see from the video, a very brutal, bloody battle. Mesa whipped Jackson, and when Jackson went for his gun, Mesa shot and killed him in a gun battle worthy of Wyatt Earp."

Dr. Wainwright says, "That Sergeant Mesa is some kind of Ranger. He risked his life to save all those people. You know, he could easily have been killed." He smiles and checks Alana's pulse and checks her bruises. "Well, Lieutenant, you are coming along quite well. We'll let you go home in a few days. I'll check on you later today."

Alana turns toward her mom and says, "Has Ranger Mesa killed anyone before this, and if so how many people?"

"Alana, Dan has been involved in several shootings. He has killed four people that I know of, including the two he shot here in Yuma. The number of people he has killed isn't as important as why he killed them. In each instance, it was to save someone else. He is not a killer. He represents the law, and everything he has done was in the line of duty."

"I know, Mom, but it is inhuman to kill so many people. I don't know if I could care about someone with so much death attached to them."

"Honey, I have news for you. Before your accident, you cared quite a lot about him. In a shootout with Jackson and his family, he was seriously injured and is still recovering from it. You stepped in front of a bullet meant for him, so it is apparent you did care about him. He is under the impression you still do. He doesn't know you've lost your memory. When he left here two days ago, he left for one reason only: to kill Jackson for what he did to you. You should have seen his face when he left. It was the face of one angry man whom I would not want to face. Alana, Daniel Mesa is one hell of a man."

Meanwhile, back in Amado, someone is crying uncontrollably.

It is six o'clock in the morning in Amado and Sonia has just brought in the newspaper. She takes a shower and goes into the kitchen for a cup of coffee when Mesha yells, "Sonia, come quickly. You have to see this." Sonia runs into the living room where Mesha is watching the news. What she sees makes her go weak in the knees. She sees the fight between Mesa and Jackson.

"Oh, my goodness, Mesha" is all she manages to say before she breaks down crying. "Mesha, he has killed another person—that makes five. Look at his face. He looks so sad. José was his best friend at one time and now he has killed him. Right or wrong he has killed someone who was like his blood brother, and this time I am not so sure he will recover. I love him dearly, and I don't know what to do."

"Girl, that man is some kind of guy," Mesha says excitedly. "He deserves all the respect and love one can muster. Sonia, if he returns, don't let him go, because if you do, he'll never come back again. I see it in his face."

In Alburquerque Dan is soaking in the tub and wondering how things got to this point. "I've killed the man who used to be my best friend. Where do I go from here? Do I remain a Ranger or do I give it up? I'd best call Alana and see how she is doing."

The phone rings in Alana's room and Adelaide answers. "Hello, Mrs. Osborne, Dan Mesa here. I'm calling to check on Alana. How is she doing?"

"Dan, she is out of the coma, but it left her unable to remember recent things. She has forgotten she knows you. Dan, I don't know what to say. The doctor says she will eventually regain her memory, but the question is when?"

Dan's heart sinks and he says, "I will leave immediately for Yuma."

Dan returns to the police station and clears up the last paperwork and prepares to leave. Lieutenant Jackson and Sergeant Laughlin tell him if he gets tired of being a Ranger, he always has a place with the Albuquerque Police Department. Dan Mesa climbs into his truck and drives west on I-40.

When Jackson's family learns of his death, Martha curses Dan Mesa and promises to get even one day. José's father shakes his head sadly and says, "Dan didn't have a choice. It was kill or be killed."

It is ten o'clock Wednesday night when Sergeant Dan Mesa walks into Alana's hospital room. It has been more than a week since she was shot. Adelaide sees him walk in and quietly walks over to him. She holds him close with tears in her eyes, saying, "You have had a hard time of it lately, and what I am about to say is going to make it even harder. Alana doesn't remember ever meeting you, and worst of all she can't remember loving you."

Daniel Mesa, Arizona Ranger, ex–air force officer, former schoolteacher, ex–rodeo cowboy, and ex-husband, suddenly finds himself more alone than ever before. Alana awakens and sees Dan.

"I assume you are Sergeant Mesa of the Rangers. I must apologize to you because I don't remember you. You appear to be a nice man. My mother told me that we were very close before my accident. I am sorry, but I don't remember you at all. I saw you on the news, and apparently this Jackson person was really a bad actor. Again I wish I could remember what we meant to each other."

Mesa shivers and fakes a smile. "I understand, ma'am." He apologizes and walks away as erect as a tree. Adelaide rushes after him.

"Dan, what will you do now? Don't give up on Alana. She will come around eventually. I still think the world of you. Please don't forget us. I will call you often and let you know how we are doing. Remember, I love you dearly, Ranger." She hugs him and kisses his cheek. Mesa turns and walks away without looking back.

Adelaide returns to Alana's room, where Alana is crying softly. Surprised, Adelaide asks, "Why are you crying?"

"There goes a good man with nowhere to go and no one to go to. If only I could remember." Adelaide hugs her daughter and understands her feelings.

Dan checks in with Major McMasters and brings him up to date. He climbs in to the 4Runner and heads back to Nogales. He arrives in Nogales at four o'clock Thursday morning and checks in with Captain Johnson.

Captain Johnson smiles and says, "It is good to see you, old friend. I've gotten the word on what happened. Dan, the colonel is well pleased, and even the governor's office has called, congratulating us and especially you on bringing this case to a successful conclusion without the additional loss of life. The Tucson newspaper wasn't kind to you, but the Phoenix and Nogales papers were very supportive. What do you plan to do now?"

"Sir, I don't know. I had planned to spend some time with Alana, but she doesn't remember me at all. It is as if these past weeks with her never occurred. I would visit Sonia, but I know she doesn't want to see me after all this. I guess I will take a few days off and try to get myself together and then return to work."

"Dan, you haven't seen your son for a while. Go and visit him for a couple of weeks."

I am thinking to myself that the captain is right. "Captain, I believe I will do that. Thanks."

When I walk into the house, the phone rings. I answer, "Hello, Mesa here."
There is a distinct whimper and then silence. The line goes dead. I have a feeling it was Sonia calling. Should I call her or just leave things as they are?

I guess I should pack for my trip to Baltimore. It will be good to see Devlin. There goes the phone again. "Hello, Mesa here." The captain is calling.

"Dan, are you flying to Maryland? The reason I asked is that while you are there, you could check in with the Richmond, Virginia, police department and find out about a prisoner they have. His name is William J. Ranson, and he's being held on a fugitive-from-justice charge. He was a material witness in a murder case and fled to save his life. The colonel wants you to escort him back. The Rangers will pay for the trip; all you have to do is escort him back."

"Captain, I have a feeling I am being had."

"No, Sergeant—well, not exactly, but we could use your expertise. Will you do it?"

I am thinking to myself how this could wind up being a total "goat rope" and how I may be the goat. "Yes, sir, I will."

"Have a good trip, Sergeant, and I will see you in a couple of weeks."

I am all packed.. I wonder how Janie is doing these days. It is time to call her.

The phone rings at the Cordon Bleu and someone answers. "Cordon Bleu, Maria speaking."

"Hello, this is Dan Mesa. May I speak to Janie Olivetti, please?"

"Please hold and I will find her for you." She leaves the phone and I wait.

Maria rushes to find Janie and says, "Janie, that Ranger is on the phone and he wants to talk to you."

Janie picks up the phone and says, "Hello, Dan. How are you? I've been keeping tabs on you since I saw you last. You've had a rough time of it."

"Janie, I am okay and I will survive. I just wanted to let you know how much I appreciate you and your friendship. I'm going east to see my son for a few days. When I return, I was wondering if you'd like to spend a few days together just having fun, just two friends who enjoy being together. I won't put any pressure on you as I did once before."

"Dan, it would be nice to spend time with you. I know how you feel about me, and I know what makes you tick and I love you for it, but I am still afraid of the big *M*. If you can put up with me, it will be great fun.

"Dan, are you recovered from your wounds? It frightened me when I heard what happened. I also saw on the news the fight between you and José. It was a brutal fight. I am sorry it had to be you who stopped him. He had to be stopped, but I don't want you to think about it too much. Remember, someone in Sierra Vista cares about you."

"I know you do, Janie. I just wish things were different. I am so tired, physically and mentally. I will call you when I get back." She is one in a million and probably the best friend a guy could have. I am quite fortunate, you know.

Janie hangs up the phone and just stands in the middle of the room smiling. Maria sees her and asks, "Why are you so happy? Does it have anything to do with that gunslinging Ranger?"

"Maria, he is not a gunslinger. He is just the greatest guy in the world, and I plan to tell him so when I see him again." She walks away as happy as can be.